Delicious Death
Madame Chalamet Ghost Mysteries 2

Byrd Nash

ROOK AND CASTLE PRESS
SAINT CHARLES, ILLINOIS

License Notes

Copyright © 2022, 2024 Byrd Nash
Editing by Emma's Edit
Cover Art by Rook and Castle Press
Published by Rook and Castle Press
All Rights Reserved.

ISBN 978-1-954811-52-2

All rights reserved. This book or any portion thereof may not be reproduced or used in any manner whatsoever without the express written permission of the publisher except for the use of brief quotations in a book review.

This book is a work of fiction. Names, characters, places, and events in this book are either products of the author's imagination or are used fictitiously. Any resemblance to actual events, places or persons, living or dead, are purely coincidental.

Byrd Nash

THIS BOOK WAS PRODUCED BY A HUMAN, NOT AI.

Publisher's Cataloging-in-Publication Data
provided by Five Rainbows Cataloging Services

Names: Nash, Byrd, author.
Title: Delicious death : a gaslamp ghost mystery / Byrd Nash.
Description: Saint Charles, IL : Rook and Castle Press, 2024. | Series: Madame Chalamet ghost mysteries.
Identifiers: ISBN 978-1-954811-51-5 (Amazon paperback) | ISBN 978-1-954811-52-2 (IngramSpark paperback) | ISBN 978-1-954811-06-5 (Kindle ebook) | ISBN 978-1-954811-12-6 (EPUB)
Subjects: LCSH: Women detectives--Fiction. | Ghosts--Fiction. | Murder--Fiction. | Fantasy fiction. | Detective and mystery stories. | Paranormal romance stories. | BISAC: FICTION / Fantasy / Gaslamp. | FICTION / Fantasy / Romance. | FICTION / Romance / Paranormal / General. | FICTION / Mystery & Detective / General. | GSAFD: Mystery fiction. | Fantasy fiction. | Occult fiction. | Love stories.
Classification: LCC PS3614.A724 D45 2022 (print) | LCC PS3614.A724 (ebook) | DDC 813/.6--dc23.

Contents

Books by Byrd Nash	vi
Chapter 1	1
Chapter 2	9
Chapter 3	19
Chapter 4	27
Chapter 5	35
Chapter 6	43
Chapter 7	53
Chapter 8	61
Chapter 9	71
Chapter 10	81
Chapter 11	91
Chapter 12	99
Chapter 13	107
Chapter 14	115
Chapter 15	125
Chapter 16	131
Chapter 17	139
Chapter 18	149
Chapter 19	157
Chapter 20	165
Author Notes	177
Cast of Characters	179

Books by Byrd Nash

Madame Chalamet Ghost Mysteries
Ghost Talker #1
Delicious Death #2
Spirit Guide #3
Gray Lady #4
Haunted Grave #5
Ghastly Mistake #6

Contemporary, Magical Realism
A Spell of Rowans

College Fae Series
Never Date a Siren #1
A Study in Spirits #2
Bane of Hounds #3

Romantic Fairytales
Dance of Hearts (Cinderella retelling)
Price of a Rose (Beauty and the Beast retelling)

Fairytale Fantasy
The Wicked Wolves of Windsor and other Fairytales

"He called it Delicious Death.
My cake! I will not have my cake called that!"
"It was a compliment really," said Miss Blacklock.
"He meant it was worth dying to eat such a cake."
A Murder is Announced, Agatha Christie

Dedications
To the son
who loved the first book
in this series.

Chapter One

Be careful what you wish for, especially during the season of the dead.

"Admit it, you're bored," said my maid and assistant, Anne-Marie.

I groaned. "There hasn't been a dead body for over a week."

"Poor you," she said with mock severity as she stripped the sheets off my bed before carrying them from the room.

How could the occasional séance to ask about Aunt Matilda's family recipes, or inquiries about lost wills, compare to the grand adventure of vanquishing a monster in the Beyond? Of course I was bored.

Sighing, I pulled back the curtain of my suite at the Crown Hotel to see that Alenbonné, port city and capital of Sarnesse, was still drowning in icy rain. Winter had arrived and with it, the dreary weather and thick fog which smothered the city in a gloomy blanket.

Behind me, there was a knock at the door, which Anne-Marie promptly answered. A female voice asked, "Is Elinor about?"

It was Dr. Charlotte LaRue, the coroner in charge of the city morgue. Maybe something interesting would happen today after all.

"Hello, Charlotte, what brings you to my side of town? However did you escape your students today?" I asked as she handed off her coat and a soaked umbrella to Anne-Marie.

"They are too busy studying for finals to pay attention to me, so I thought I'd come and demand that you treat me to lunch."

Charlotte was in her fifties; a thin, wiry woman with an oval face, a beaky nose, and prominent brown eyes. Today she wore her usual about-town mannish outfit of trousers, vest, and frock coat. The fabric was a gray tweed with a stock tie of small gray dots on a field of black.

"We can catch up on the gossip," she said, rubbing her chilled hands briskly.

The Crown Hotel was one of three luxury hotels in Alenbonné that offered residency suites. My suite included a main bedroom with an attached bathroom, a sitting room, a kitchenette, and a small room for a personal servant. Most meals I took in their banquet hall; when it was closed, I dined out or had a light tea in my suite.

Charlotte and I chatted as we made our way down the carpeted stairs. It was past the prime lunch hour and the main lobby was quiet, with only a few of the regulars reading newspapers in their favorite chairs.

"There's been a shocking lack of dead bodies," was Dr. LaRue's comment and her carrying voice, along with her unconventional outfit for a woman, received a few outraged male stares from behind rustling papers.

"I was complaining about the same thing myself," I confided, more quietly. "So boring that no one of interest has died in some violent, horrible manner in these past few months."

Tall, narrow windows lined one wall of the Crown's dining room, facing the street. The rain glazed the windows to gray, and it was no surprise that not even a newsboy was braving the wet promenade today.

"Let's sit by the fireplace and shake off some of the damp," I suggested.

The hotel's massive hearth gave off a cheerful warmth, and the paneled walls of deep mahogany wood, despite the size of the room, made for a cozy spot. The head waiter handed us cards printed with the day's specials.

"Where is everyone today, Pierre? I thought the restaurant would be busy?"

"Many are taking lunch in their rooms, madame."

"Is there any mulled wine to be had today?"

"Oh, yes, madame. Shall I bring you some?"

We both nodded agreement, and after he left with our orders, Charlotte and I got down to a good chat.

"Haven't seen Inspector Barbier for at least a month." The doctor spoke in her habitual abrupt way. "Thinking the guardia might be ailing, I stopped by the gendarmes to check on him. Barbier is as bored as we— said it's all been domestic incidents. Being cooped indoors really brings out the nasty at home, but nothing really juicy for us to sink our teeth in."

I asked, "Do you think it's pathetic that we wish people would die for our entertainment?"

"Not pathetic at all! Some might call it ghoulish, but those are ordinary people living dull lives."

It wasn't long before pewter mugs filled with spiced wine, a warm soup starter, and a basket of rolls made it to our table. Pierre glided away, a majestic black swan, to take care of another table.

"It's the anniversary, isn't it?" asked Charlotte, while looking around the room as if there was a spy who might overhear us.

"Twelve years ago, last Wednesday."

"Has Barbier made any progress with your father's murder?"

"No, I'm afraid not. Whatever the reason, my father's watch was in the Hells turned out to be a dead end."

"Frustrating."

Barbier and I had bonded that awful day twelve years ago. After discovering my father, I'd run into the street, screaming for help, and it had been Barbier, walking down the street as a sergeant, who had responded to my pleas. While the other gendarmes had fallen away from the case over the years, he stubbornly kept working it. I think he felt it was his first big case, and not having a resolution to it was a personal insult.

For some reason I couldn't explain, I had not shared with him or Charlotte the tale that the watch had told me through psychometry. The thought that someone he knew had murdered my father was too raw. Besides, psychometry would not stand up in a court of law. I needed hard evidence, a confession, a suspect.

"That's a hullabaloo back there. Did someone send back their meal?"

At the doctor's words, I finally paid attention to the noisy racket happening behind the swinging door that led back to the kitchen. Before I could answer, Henri Colbert, the manager of the Crown, was at our table. Usually impeccable both in manner and address, he now appeared flustered.

"Madame Chalamet." His tone spoke of urgency and privacy, as he cleared his throat before saying in a strained voice, "There is a disagreement in the kitchen. Between Chef Perdersen and his companion."

Before he could say anything further, a saucepan came flying through the double doors and landed with a thud on the carpet. The few diners in the hall stopped eating and stared at the cookware in stunned disbelief. A rush of excited chatter followed.

"I would be happy to serve as mediator," I told Colbert hastily. Placing my napkin to the side of my plate, I told Charlotte to wait for me before following him to the entrance to the kitchen. There, he paused.

"It wouldn't help for me to enter. Claude always feels it is my fault that their love affair ended."

"No need for you to do so. I can manage him on my own."

A look of relief passed over his face. "Thank you, Madame Chalamet."

I pushed open the door and walked into a shouting match.

"You don't love me!"

It was the same story as old. The temperamental Claude Frossard was up to his old tricks, trying to make the head chef of the Crown, Gerhard Perdersen, feel guilty that he had a life.

"Viktor needed to know how many eggs to order!" This retort was rather muffled, for it came from under the worktable, where master chef extraordinaire Gerhard had sought sanctuary. At his words, a meat cleaver came down heavily, sticking itself into the butcher block counter.

"I saw how you looked at him!"

"Claude, why would you think that?"

At my question, Claude turned to me and burst into tears, wailing. His arms flew over his head in a frantic, desperate plea. "He's leaving. Did you know that? Leaving the Crown!"

"I'm sure you're wrong about that, Claude. Mysir Gerhard loves being here."

While Claude might be a ghost, when he threw one of his temper tantrums, his form became as substantial as anyone living. He was a very handsome young man in his late twenties, frozen at the age at which he had committed suicide. Black hair fell over his forehead and he swept it back with a dramatic hand gesture, lifting his chin as he informed me, "He has a wandering eye. I should know."

I didn't want to get into an argument about who was right about something that had happened three years ago, when Gerhard made the mistake of kissing someone other than Claude. Yes, it had ended Claude's life, and it had been horrible; but on the other hand, wasn't terrorizing Gerhard for years enough retribution?

Perhaps if Claude hadn't died when he was young, his ghost

would have a better perspective about life. But then again, spirits gained power from extreme emotions, and it was his possessive jealousy that prevented him from traveling to the Afterlife. Instead, as a Noise Ghost, he made random appearances in the earthly plane to torment Gerhard, forcing the chef to regret having a fling with a sous chef twenty years his junior.

"He's not leaving the Crown," I stated firmly.

From under the table, Gerhard contradicted me. "But I am, Madame Chalamet."

Shocked at his desertion and the idea of no longer having access to my favorite dessert, it took me a moment to register the flurry of pots and pans that leapt from their hooks, smashing to the tile floor and making my ears ring. Generally, a Ghost Talker lets a Noise Ghost spend the energy they've gathered from the living. However, in a professional kitchen, there were far too many knives about. Someone could seriously get hurt.

"Explain yourself, chef!" I shouted over the din.

"It's for the royal competition! The Winter Revels!"

Oh, well, that explained everything. This year, the annual arts and skills competition sponsored by King Guénard was going to feature cooking. "He's only leaving for the contest. You heard him, Claude. He'll be back."

"No, he won't! He'll find another to love." The ghost was sobbing now, but at least it had stopped throwing things. It was winding down like a tired clock nearing the end.

"Claude? Do you remember when you fell in love with Gerhard? Wasn't it in the summer?"

"No. It was the spring. The cherry trees were blooming when I applied to work here at the Crown."

Ghosts followed patterns, and it was best for everyone to get Claude back to his old, comfortable memories, which held far more of a grip on his spirit than current events.

"Remember how you admired him?" I prompted.

"More than anyone. I had met no one like him before— his energy. He cooked like a madman on fire. Such passion."

The ghost lost himself in his reminiscences, and the solidity of his form frayed, the power maintaining his manifestation fading. I gestured for Gerhard to come out from under the table.

"Did he feel the same way?"

"I think so. I can't remember."

Forgetting wasn't unusual. As time passed, ghosts lost the ability to hold their memories, a dementia that we often see in the living, and a process greatly accelerated in the dead. The older the ghost, the less it really remembered.

"I'm sure Gerhard remembers, don't you, chef?"

Prompted by me, Perdersen knew what to say. After all, these scenes between him and the Noise Ghost were the reason I could afford a suite at the Crown; my job being to calm Claude down so Gerhard could work his magic with food. They had first asked me to sunder him, a process to vanquish a ghost from all three planes. When I'd pointed out that would destroy Claude's soul and prevent it from reaching the Afterlife, Gerhard had changed his mind.

"Claude Frossard was the most handsome assistant I ever had. I couldn't take my eyes off of him. How he trembled when I touched his hand holding the soup ladle..."

There was a sigh, a light breeze stirred my hair, and Claude expired, snuffed out until the next time it sucked up enough energy to cause chaos again.

"He's gone."

At my words, Gerhard gave a heavy sigh and started shaking his head, throwing his hands up. "When will Claude give up? It's been three years already."

"Was there something that set him off?" I asked.

"Viktor was asking about the egg order. He's one of our suppliers. He touched my arm, and then Claude exploded." Gerhard rubbed his bald pate with both hands.

It was sometimes hard to reconcile Claude's glowing description of his lover with Gerhard. He had jowls, even a double chin, and small raisin eyes, but I had seen him in command of the kitchen, so understood Claude's infatuation. The man transformed when preparing food; he was a general leading the charge when it was the dinner hour. An artist consumed by his talent who produced food fit for royalty.

"Tell me about the Winter Revels. When will you be leaving?"

The king's Winter Revels were an annual competition held to highlight various artists and trades. Last year it had been painters, and the year before that, silversmiths.

"I was leaving next Tuesday."

"I'd suggest going as soon as possible. Claude's spirit should be quiet for about a week, not much longer."

"But what if he comes back when Chef is gone?" This question was from Henri, who had crept into the kitchen. The rest of the kitchen staff trickled in and started cleaning up the mess Claude had left behind, taking pots off the gas burners and retrieving knives from the floor.

"Just tell him that Chef is not here, but don't imply he is gone for long. Speak as if he just stepped away and could return at any time. Ghosts find it hard to keep track of time like we do. Hopefully, that will keep him confused enough until the competition is over. Come find me if he causes any trouble."

At the swinging door, I turned around and added to Henri, "It's not like I'm busy."

Chapter Two

A break in the soggy weather the next day made me eager to try my new two-wheeled riding machine. The sales clerk in the showroom had told me it was the latest in mechanical engineering while I stroked my hand down the cool steel all painted in bright red, with white lettering: Lady's Safety Edition.

"Perfectly safe," the clerk assured me, not knowing my profession or that I worked with the gendarmes to solve murders. Regardless, I bought it and the vision of being able to move around the city without paying fees for quick-cabs and imagining the breeze against my face as I sailed along the canals, pedaling smoothly, while covering long distances with ease.

The thing took more balance than I thought, so I practiced for weeks in the ruelle, a block over from the hotel. The stable boys paused from their work to either cheer me on or laugh heartily, depending on if I was staying on or falling off. When I was on more than off, I left the alley and ventured out to the pavement, at first only in the early morning hours when there were fewer pedestrians.

Wheeling it out from a storage shed at the back of the Crown,

I walked it across the street to the park that ran along the canal. Steadying myself, I mounted, only showing a hint of my shapely ankle. Unfortunately, there was no grumpy man with cynical eyes and black hair to admire my poised seat and upright carriage as I pedaled along.

I had quickly learned that liberal use of my bell on the handlebars helped to remind pedestrians to let me pass on the promenade. I crossed the humpback bridge, and seeing an acquaintance who was sitting outside at a café table gave a wave, an act that wobbled my front end. He returned a salute.

The sun was out and as I turned to enter the park, I quickly took evasive action to avoid a courting couple who were too involved with each other to hear my bell. Next, I turned right and then a sharp left, to go between a nanny pushing a baby carriage, and a man walking his dog. The dog leaped up in excitement, but his leash stopped him, and I was past them before the little terror could think to grab my skirt with his teeth.

There was a gentle rise, and I pushed hard down on pedals, feeling the machine under me work hard. At the top of the hill was a small courtyard, the center of which was a circular fountain featuring a statue of a water nymph riding a dolphin. A child was sailing paper boats on one side, while a group of young ladies were tossing coins and making wishes on the other. Everyone was out, enjoying the break in the weather.

I swept around the circle and went down a path that started downhill. This was a sharp descent, and I started to brake gently to slow the machine down. Looking ahead, I sucked in my breath, catching sight of the Duke de Archambeau and his sister, Lady Valentina Fontaine. The two were standing in the middle of the walkway, and looked to be arguing.

I hadn't seen him since our last case resolved. Now, here he was!

Surprised, I let up on the pedals and forgot to ring the bell. The machine accelerated like a horse given the bit. There was a flash of a white face and startled eyes before Lady Valentina opted for the safety of the grass. Meanwhile, the duke took the full collision of my bicycle with his back. Since boulders do not bounce, I sadly lost the day.

"Madame Chalamet, may I assist you?" The duke's voice was politely detached, as if he was asking a poor relation to partner him at a dance held at an inferior establishment.

As I gripped the duke's hand to stand up, I heard a ripping sound. The chain held my skirt! So much for the safety guard; the manufacturer would get a strongly worded letter and a bill for damages tomorrow.

"Stop moving. You're making it worse," commanded the duke. He bent down to untangle the hem of my skirt. "You're free now, but I fear your machine isn't in good shape."

Sadly, I looked down to find the front wheel crooked and bent. How would I get it back to the Crown?

"Tristan!" said Lady Valentina, who was being helped to her feet by a passing stranger.

He ignored her, asking me, "Are you hurt? That was quite a tumble."

"No, I'm fine."

This meeting threw me into confusion, and I felt myself blushing. The last time we had seen each other was two months ago after solving the mystery of the king's tiara, and this wasn't the meeting I had fabricated in my mind. It was supposed to take place with me wearing an elegant evening dress and greeting him with a smooth laugh. Instead, I looked an absolute fright, with grass and grease stains on my skirt and my hair trailing down my back.

As usual, *he* was impeccable in his turnout. Walking coat, frock coat, trousers, and vest, all tailored to perfection. His snow-white cravat was tied in the square knot style known as The Intellectual.

Lady Valentina came to his side and possessively put her arm within his own. "Since Madame Chalamet says she is fine, can we continue our way through the park? Or does she want to knock us down again?"

Archambeau absentmindedly patted her arm before dropping it.

"I think I must help a lady in distress, Valentina. I doubt she can get this thing home in the condition it is now." Stepping to the curb, he hailed a passing quick-cab. As it pulled up, the duke asked me, "Are you still at the Crown Hotel, Madame Chalamet?"

"Yes. Yes, I am."

One royal coin, joined with a few others, exchanged hands. "Would you take Madame Chalamet's damaged vehicle to the Crown Hotel?"

"Eh?" said the man. Archambeau pointed to the Lady's Safety Edition bicycle, now sadly crumpled, and, at the emergence of more coins, he speedily climbed down from his perch. In a moment, the two men had the bicycle on the back of the quick-cab.

I moved to leave with it, but the duke stopped me.

"Even a brave Ghost Talker must feel rattled after taking such a tumble. Come and sit with us before you return home. You can entertain us with tales about your latest haunts."

Perhaps I would have said no, but the anger on Lady Valentina's face at her brother's words made me agree. Taking my arm with one of his own, and using the other for his sister, we left the park, crossing the street to the other side, to the café district.

He stopped at one and found us a table. Within seconds of us being seated, a waiter promptly appeared. Perhaps he recognized the duke, or maybe it was the expensive tailoring which gained us such exceptional service. Regardless of the reason, our table soon boasted hot tea and coffee.

"Put some sugar in that, Chalamet," the duke ordered, and before I could comply, he dropped a cube into my cup and gave it a swirl with one of his own spoons. Normally I would have protested Archambeau's high-handedness, but with a hot drink in front of me, I realized that sitting down felt good. The accident had shaken me more than I'd realized.

Some thin lemon biscuits appeared, as well as toasted bread points and a soft creamy cheese flavored with fresh herbs. It all was delicious, but this spread of hospitality did not appease Lady Valentina. She refused to sit down, even as more plates, knives, cups, and food continued to appear.

"I shall make my way home alone, then," she said loftily.

Scraping a generous portion of cheese across a piece of toasted bread, the duke replied calmly, "That would probably be best. I shall see to Madame Chalamet."

"I will let Mother know what delayed you."

"Do whatever you think best, Valentina."

The woman left, her back as flat as a brick, and I couldn't stop myself from saying when she was out of earshot, "I hope I didn't make your quarrel worse with my appearance."

"I see your powers of observation remain as keen as ever, Chalamet, though perhaps not powerful enough to avoid hitting people walking a public footpath."

I bit my lip, unsure whether he was teasing or chastising me. He had not reached out to me since the Giles Monet affair, and naturally, I had not inquired about him. The difference of our stations, the lack of a blood or family relationship, made it unseemly that I send him a note. News of him in the papers said he was a guest at a party or attended the theater. Nothing substantial or interesting.

Perhaps he sensed my uncertainty, for he gave me one measuring glance and relented. "Valentina is busy spreading rumors about my late wife, Minette."

Ah, Minette. His late wife whom he had murdered.

Thinking of his sister's behavior during the dinner party held at the duke's residence, Hartwood House, I said, trying to be fair, "Lady Fontaine didn't strike me as a rumor monger."

Instead of tea, the duke was drinking a black coffee. His fingers stroked the mug's white ceramic handle, and I noticed with surprise that he no longer wore his wedding band.

"When it comes to my dead wife, my sister has little diplomacy. She and Minette had an acrimonious relationship. She resented having her duties as hostess given over to Minette upon my marriage, and Minette couldn't stop reminding her that as a sister-in-law who was without a husband or children, Valentina had no authority over her or the house."

"I imagine it's hard to be in charge and suddenly find yourself deposed only because of a marriage of convenience."

I don't know if he choked or was trying to suppress a laugh. When he recovered, the duke said, "That's what I've missed, madame, your blunt speaking. Bare-knuckle punches."

When I opened my mouth, he added, "Don't apologize. I rather enjoy your frankness."

"I wasn't about to. I was going to ask why your sister would care enough to spread rumors about a dead enemy."

"Probably in an attempt to dissuade any women I might meet from becoming interested in a longer relationship. As long as I am unmarried, she retains domestic control of Hartwood when our mother is at Chambaux. She and Lady Baudelaire have been telling others that my dead wife is knocking women down my stairs in some sort of ghostly revenge. It has dissuaded social invitations, as you can imagine."

"Now Lady Baudelaire I believe! She's nasty enough to do that, and she does not like you at all. Remember that Ghost Hunt she made me do?"

He gave me that half smile I remembered. Archambeau had a strange way of smiling. It would start slowly, but before it would complete, it faded away. "I'm glad my troubles have cheered you up. You look better since your fall. Not so pale, and the gears are moving behind your eyes again."

"But you don't really want to be back doing the society

rounds, dancing to the tune of the Buttons-and-Bows marriage market again, do you?" I protested, curious.

"No. But neither do I want any woman I meet to start like a frightened horse, because they think I'm haunted by my dead wife." He paused and took a sip from his cup before saying, "Go ahead; I sense you have something that you wish to tell me. Something you fear I won't like." He raised a finger. "Remember, though, I'm strong enough to withstand the impact of a runaway bicycle."

Swallowing, I decided to risk it. "It wasn't my business at the time, but I couldn't help but notice—."

"Naturally, you being a noticing sort of person," he replied, smirking.

"That the fall down the stairs by one of your guests last year was probably intentional. When I stayed at your house, I found a nail and evidence that someone stretched a wire across the top step."

His intelligent gray eyes went from lazy and amused to sharp and dangerous. "Perhaps I did that to rid myself of a troublesome house guest that had overstayed her welcome?"

"I think you would just hail them a coach and kick them out the door. That seems more your style. Besides, you weren't in the house during that episode."

"However did you know I wasn't at home? No, wait." His powerful fingers gave a loud snap. "Let me guess, your maidservant. What was her name?"

"Anne-Marie. And please don't hold her investigation against her, but if I had not given her something to do, she would have grown quite bored during our stay at your house. And when bored, she gets into dreadful mischief. She steals newsboy's caps, or tells the hotel staff wildly exaggerated tales about my ghosts."

"Hm. So no ghost pushed Lady Annabel van den Berg down the stairs? Thank you for that information. I shall look into it."

From his closed-off expression, I could tell that any further discussion on this matter was done. I cast around for something else to speak about, and since it was on my mind because of yesterday's incident in the Crown's kitchen, I asked, "Are you going to the Winter Revels?"

"Of course. King Guénard requires me there."

I wondered why. To defend the king against a thrown pie or a fruit tart? Perhaps he read my surprise, for he added, "My presence is purely ceremonial due to being the landholder of Chambaux, one of the largest estates in Sarnesse. It will be a tedious assignment, at best."

"Really? To stay at a country villa, eating creations made by the best chefs in Sarnesse? You have a strange idea of what causes tedium, Your Grace. Sounds lovely to me."

Archambeau said, "If it would interest you, ask King Guénard for an invitation."

"I couldn't send a note to him requesting an invitation. That would be intrusive and arrogant."

"After what you did in saving his treaty? Single-handedly finding the tiara while I gaped at some dancing girl? You were the heroine of the hour. King Guénard owes you a reward."

"Does that grate? Me outsmarting the creature, not you?"

"Madame Chalamet!" He smiled, a full one this time. "You do like to whittle a man's ego down, don't you? It will take an exceptional man to consider marriage with you. Someone with a robust constitution that can withstand crashing bicycles and being possessed by ghosts."

I laughed. "I have no plans to marry, so that will not be a problem."

His coffee mug paused on the way to his lips. Archambeau cocked his head, eyebrows raised, clearly disbelieving me. "None?"

"As a free woman of twenty-nine years, I am in control of my destiny. Yes, I have bank managers, who, being men, must serve as guardians for my money due to silly laws that think women are no brighter than sheep, but they are far easier to persuade than a husband would be! In the eyes of the law, marriage would make me a possession, placing my inheritance and income under my husband's control."

"I'm sure anyone you marry would be generous with an allowance."

His words made me choke on my tea. "Generous with my own money? I think not! Besides, it's not all about money, mysir de duke. It's about the loss of my freedom. To come and go as I please. To make friends with who I want instead of being told by a husband who is acceptable."

He seemed taken aback. "I'm sorry. I didn't realize you felt that strongly about it."

I was not going to lecture him, but through the course of my work, I had seen too many women enter relationships which became a prison. Stripped of autonomy, left at home, while their husband did what he wanted. Begging for money to feed their children or clothe themselves. There were too many women in the morgue that if they had forgone a relationship with a man would still be alive.

Unaware of my dark thoughts, he continued. "I cannot imagine a man holding you back, madame, regardless of your marital state. Or what the law dictates. You would step outside convention. Don't tell me you wouldn't."

"I am sure you are right, mysir de duke, but why be the moon in a household when you can be the sun?" I tried for a light tone, trying to shake away the image of dead women and their souls marking my heart with their Ghost Talks.

"Perhaps to your husband, you *would* be the sun. I've heard poets say this is so."

Bursting out laughing, I said, "Can you imagine anything worse than being married to a poet? I don't think you were very fond of being possessed by Bastiaan Hagen."

Cup in hand, staring thoughtfully at the ceiling, he said, "Do you know, I often find myself rhyming words without meaning to."

I laughed while I stood to take my leave. "Thank you for taking care of my bicycle, but I must get to an appointment."

"Another ghost to chat with, madame?"

"No, I am going over my investments at the bank. Unfortunately, the law still forces me to seek their advice every quarter if I wish access to my inheritance, even though my father's been dead for over a decade."

"A tedious chore you could forgo and let a husband let handle for you while you enjoyed a visit to your dressmaker to buy a new hat."

"And discover he had run off with his mistress and my money, leaving me bankrupt? No thank you, Your Grace. As a Ghost Talker, I've seen behind the curtain and marriage is not for me."

Chapter Three

The next day, I was curled up on a chair in my suite at the Crown when there was a polite tap. Anne-Marie was home nursing her sick mother, so I answered it. One of the hotel footmen was holding a small tray with a thick envelope sitting on top.

"This just came for you, madame," he said. Thanking him, I retreated inside.

I didn't recognize the handwriting, but the seal on the back displayed the royal coat of arms. Excited, I broke the wax seals, and two cards fluttered to the ground. The note read, after all the polite salutations: "—it has come to the attention of His Majesty that Madame Chalamet would enjoy attending the Winter Revels in Vouvant."

I did a little pirouette and waltzed around the furniture, thinking of what I'd heard about the land of wine, lemons, and olives. And sun, blessed sun, during the winter.

Dr. Charlotte LaRue accompanied me as my guest.

An hour into the trip, our train crossed the Vallée des Larmes river, leaving the grayness of Alenbonné skies behind. From here, we would continue south and away from the sea, taking us to a broad valley with a more temperate clime. As gray skies gave way to blue, my mood lightened.

"Look," I said, pointing out the window to the town that was being revealed in the distance.

"That's Vouvant? Never been there. What do we know of it?"

Opening the pamphlet I had brought from Alenbonné, I read out loud, "Each year, the Winter Revels rotate between the estates owned by the king's noble subjects. This year, Count Christoffer Westergaard's villa, Lindengaard, has the honor—"

"Honor? More like open your bank book! The expense of entertaining the king must be stupendous. Our king, the moocher," interjected Charlotte.

"Charlotte, be nice! Please try to remember that it was a courtesy to me he allowed me to bring a guest."

"Oh, I always forget that you've met him."

"Only briefly."

"Well, he doesn't know me from the cat on the street."

"But he will get to know you— that's the point of the Winter Revels. He will mingle and meet his subjects. They'll be all sorts of people, both high and low."

Charlotte sprawled her long, trousered legs in front of her. She had brought a pipe today and was tapping it down as she spoke. "I know one thing they will all have in common."

"What?"

"Trying to spoil my holiday. As soon as they discover I'm a doctor, they'll ask for free medical advice while I'm working my way through a buttered crab. But I've found a failsafe method for dealing with it. I'll listen very carefully, give my thoughts, and the next day send them a bill."

"Is that why you brought your medical bag?"

"Of course! There are always fainting ladies who tied their

corsets too tight. A whiff or two of smelling salts, and a listen to their heart, bring me at least twenty royals. How else do you think I can afford my skiing holidays to Zulskaya?"

I burst out laughing. "Oh, Charlotte!"

"Don't 'oh, Charlotte' me! I see you brought your own valise. Full of spirit-talking concoctions and a man-stopper, I'm guessing. You are as ready as I am."

"Ghosts are everywhere," I said primly.

"As is illness."

"Sometimes they go hand-in-hand."

"Speaking of which, you should consider becoming an alienist, Elinor. It's obvious you have a talent for treating mind illnesses. It's a lucrative business. Got a friend down at a seaside resort who told me he rakes in the royals after a day holding the hands of rich ladies who have the vapors."

"I admit that exploring mind-diseases fascinates me, but I'll stay with the Morpheus Society for now. Though I wish they would see how this new field exploring the mind could complement our work."

"Rejected it, have they?" Charlotte leaned back on the blue velvet seat and started drawing on her pipe. The rich tobacco scent filled the air.

"I think they fear the competition and alternative ways of approaching the problem. Parnell Lafayette—"

"Lafayette? Is he still a thorn in your side? Never forgiven you for that prank of putting chickens in his bed when you both were in training, has he?"

I grimaced. "He's very powerful in the Society's hierarchy now. I can't think why; he insults more than he praises."

"In my experience, some patients prefer the doctor who is rough with them. Bucks them up. Makes them feel like they are really suffering."

Trying to see the brighter side of things, I told her, "I'm working on a paper about the ghost-dragon incident and presenting it at the next annual meeting. Usually ghosts produce only a simulacrum from their own experiences, and the living is unable to influence it. Somehow, though, I could bring my man-stopper into a space it created from my memories. We thought such a thing was impossible!"

Charlotte was always up to debate. "I didn't think it was safe for the living to stay in the Beyond."

"That's true. Mediums who have spent too long there have returned with their minds altered. A few have gone insane. I was lucky to escape with all my wits intact." Thinking of the sanitorium the Morpheus Society kept for those mentally lost after lingering too long in a place only for ghosts, I grew serious. "The creature used my memories to make it look like the conservatory at Hartwood, the duke's townhome. I don't know how. But it drained the energy from two people to keep the simulacrum in place."

Before I could say more, the door to our carriage slid open and a striking young woman entered. "May I share a seat with you, ladies?"

I promptly stood up, giving her my own, and took the one next to Charlotte.

The newcomer was breathing shallowly and her pale face was flushed, as if she had a fever. Even agitated, she moved with a fluid grace, a sign of the stern school of etiquette of the upper class; and from the expensive refinement of her dress, cloak, and hat, was a woman with access to money and taste.

Taking in her pale face, my friend gave a victorious look at me. "See? My first client!"

"Please don't faint," I begged the newcomer. "Dr. LaRue charges twenty royals to revive you from a swoon, which is grossly overpriced for just a whiff of ammonia."

"It's a thriving niche business," insisted Charlotte.

"Are you often called upon to revive ladies?" the newcomer asked Charlotte, curiosity replacing fright.

"I had eight fainting ladies last semester. They bring their beaus to my autopsies just so they can collapse into handsome arms."

"Autopsies?" squeaked our guest, clearly shocked.

"This is Dr. Charlotte LaRue, coroner of Alenbonné. I'm Madame Elinor Chalamet."

"I'm Lady Tulip Langenberg."

Saying her name, she cast a fearful glance to the window in the door, where the shadowy outline of a man passed by our compartment. I left my seat and pulled the shade down, and turned the lock to alert passengers in the aisle that our train carriage was full. Lady Tulip's shoulders relaxed at the click of the sign's lever.

Charlotte asked bluntly, "Are all the Langenbergs saddled with flower names?"

"Only myself. I'm an only child, you see, and both of my parents are deceased."

"Not recently, in some horrible way, I trust?" asked Charlotte, showing a bit too much eagerness.

"My mother died in childbirth, and my father a few years ago in a boating accident."

The doctor's resulting disappointment at hearing about these ordinary deaths was almost comical. I rushed in to explain. "Excuse my companion's manner, Lady Langenberg. She sometimes lets her enthusiasm for her job interfere with her social encounters." Changing the subject, I asked, "Are you headed to the Winter Revels?"

"Yes." Her voice was growing stronger now, and she gave us a pretty smile. I guessed her age at about twenty; not much older, with that smooth, dewy complexion. "If you have never been there, I promise you it is an enchanting beauty spot— an ideal choice for walks, fishing, and tasting the wines of the region."

"You are familiar with it?"

"Yes, very familiar. My family visits here every winter. We are distant relations to Count Westergaard, who is the landowner of

Lindengaard." Suddenly, her eyes, large ones with a blue that could almost be called violet, widened. "Now I recall where I've heard of you. Are you *the* Madame Chalamet? The Ghost Talker?"

Ah. This type of interest always resulted in a request.

"Yes, I am she."

Her gaze grew intent. "I have heard of you from Jacques Moreau. That you are a very understanding person and helpful to those in need."

"Jacques and I are old childhood friends. Are you in need of help, or do you know a friend who is?"

Her sigh was as light as a feather. "I am being followed."

"By a man?"

She blinked. "How did you know?"

"You are very beautiful," said Charlotte bluntly.

Her long eyelashes swept over her violet eyes in modest confusion. She said faintly, "You are right that it is a man. He is pressing his suit."

"And you do not favor him." My statement wasn't a question, but she answered it as if it was.

"No, I do not. He has been chasing me up and down this train, trying to catch me alone. I fear he has bribed my maid, though perhaps I do her a disservice. But at the last moment, she professed to being severely ill. After I left her on the train platform to board, he appeared. I do not believe it was a coincidence."

"I see." Indeed I did. A young woman, alone, to be assaulted and compromised would cause a quick marriage to save face for the family. An orphan would have no parent to advocate for her. What were her guardians thinking to have left her so vulnerable? "Does this man have a name?"

She swallowed, and her gloved hands in her lap fluttered weakly, like a dying butterfly.

"Lord Jansen Buckard. We met when I was visiting a charity hospital. I thought him charming at the time. His thinking was so in line with my own principles to help the poor that I felt an immediate fellow feeling existed between us. When I later learned the best social circles had rejected him, he insisted it was due to youthful indiscretions, long in his past."

She paused; a small tear escaped down the corner of her lashes. "But I have since learned that he well-deserves his reputation. To think I once believed him, championed him to my friends—"

Charlotte summed up Lord Buckard with one word. "Cad."

Lady Tulip stopped again, her lips trembling, before she continued her story. "When I was still in Alenbonné, something strange happened. I do not know if Lord Buckard was behind it, but a note came for me. It purported to be from a friend of mine and begged me to meet her at the park at a certain time. When I went, two men tried to force me into a waiting carriage. Luckily, a city guardia heard my screams and came to my assistance. They fled when they heard his whistle."

"Blackguard!" said Charlotte. I saw her grip the top of her cane, which concealed a swordstick.

I handed Lady Landenberg a handkerchief from my pocket. She dabbed at the corner of her eyes and continued her story. "Since then, I fear I'm followed wherever I go."

"Describe Lord Buckard," I commanded.

"He is fair, his hair a curly blond. Brown eyes. He has a mustache and an onyx ring on his left hand. He is strong, tall and athletic; if he lays hands on me, I cannot hope to be free of him, that I am sure of."

I had already pulled down my valise and was removing my man-stopper from one of the inner compartments. "If he finds us, there is no need to worry about your safety."

Chapter Four

I loaded my gun, thinking over a plan on how to rescue the girl. "If we can get you out of the train station safely, what will you do?"

"My uncle, Viscount Klass Melgraeve, is already at Lindengaard waiting for me."

"Which begs the question, why you didn't travel with him?"

She flushed, this time with anger. "He did not allow it."

"Do you think he will protect you?"

She bit her lip. "Once I would have thought yes, but now, I'm not so sure. But King Guénard will be there, and he is my godfather. I plan on begging for his help in the matter."

Hopefully, she could convince the king, for otherwise the girl had little choice. This was the fate of young women without a means to support themselves: beholden to their male relatives for protection and guidance. Shamed by society for any misstep.

Charlotte asked me, "What's your plan, Elinor?"

"We should pull into the station at any moment, so we need to be quick." I pulled down Charlotte's case and sorted through her clothes, tossing a shirt, waistcoat, jacket, and trousers to the young woman. "Your dress will give the game away, Lady Langenberg. Change. I'll wear your outfit and act as a decoy."

You could gauge the level of the young lady's fright by the quickness with which she hastily unbuttoned her dress without protesting the unsuitability of wearing the doctor's mannish clothes. She wasn't as thin as Charlotte, but she was about the same height, and small-chested. The doctor's garments weren't a bad fit.

Sadly, I had neither the willowy form of the lady nor the whipcord thinness of Dr. LaRue. At five foot two, I was probably a good six inches shorter than Lady Langenberg. I put on the highest heels I could find in my luggage, and she changed her footwear to something out of Charlotte's baggage. But my rounded curves caused problems, and I had to continue wearing my blouse under her dress, with a gap three fingers wide at the back.

"Don't worry. I'll stitch it up," promised Charlotte.

"With what?"

Instead of answering, she opened her medical bag and started threading a needle. She did a quick whip-stitch as the train slowed, approaching the Vouvant station.

"Not perfect. Don't put any strain on it. This fabric is far too thin to hold my rough stitches."

"No pockets! You must have your seamstress put pockets in your dresses, Lady Langenberg." I gave my pistol to Charlotte just in case our plan did not work and they had to defend themselves. Lady Langenberg's hat covered most of my dusky blond hair, and her blue wool cloak concealed Charlotte's stitchery.

Meanwhile, a spare hat from Charlotte covered the girl's shiny brown curls. By pulling up her coat collar, we concealed the womanly bun at the back of her neck. Handing her the doctor's case, I said, "Hold it like this and let it bump against your thigh. It might help disguise your gait."

The train pulled to a stop, and in moments shadows passed

our door of passengers already disembarking. We would need to hurry.

"Charlotte, I spotted a group of students three doors down from ours. Can you two merge into their group? I don't know, though, how you will get to Lindengaard—"

Lady Tulip said eagerly, "Count Westergaard will have coaches at the train stop for all the Winter Revel visitors. He is a very genial host."

Charlotte nodded. "Don't worry about us. We will be fine. What about you?"

"I'll distract Lord Buckard and then catch up with you at Lindengaard."

With our plan in place, I left the carriage first, wrapping the cloak around me and keeping my head in the back of the hood. In a moment, the other two exited, heading the opposite way to mingle with students who were probably coming home to enjoy the winter break. With satisfaction, I saw the two women quickly get swallowed in a sea of black and brown men's coats.

I pushed against the stream of people, looking into carriage cars and out windows, trying to gain a glimpse of my quarry. I found Lord Buckard standing on the train platform, scanning the crowd. He was exactly as Lady Tulip described: an exceedingly handsome man who stood with a godlike arrogance. He repulsed me. But perhaps to a younger woman, his air of superiority would have been attractive.

Traveling down the aisle of several more cars, I dismounted where I could be sure my back would be to Lord Buckard. Over my shoulder, I watched him until he spotted me. As soon as he did, I grabbed handfuls of loose skirt and started weaving in and out of the crowd, displaying only my back to his pursuit.

Thankfully, the porters moving the cases and boxes off the train helped to delay him. Shoving them out of the way with a muttered oath, he gained on me quickly.

When I was passing through the ticket station building, his

fingers dug in like a claw and spun me about. He was a man in a full rage: hard stones for eyes and a naturally pale complexion now flushed, with flared nostrils and a thinly compressed mouth. A man ready for violence.

Seeing my face, he exclaimed in outraged surprise, "You aren't Lady Tulip!"

"Who?" I asked innocently.

For a moment I thought I'd carried it off, but he grabbed the front of the cloak and flipped the edge back.

"You must know Lady Langenberg, to be wearing her dress. Where is she, damn you?!" He seized my arms and brought me to his chest, a hawk holding a songbird. As he shook me, I found it hard to breathe.

Gasping, I choked out, "She is none of your concern, mysir!"

"You—"

A voice I sometimes heard in my nightmares demanded, "What is going on here?"

For a moment, I thought Lord Buckard had lost his mind to his rage, for he snarled back at the Duchesse de Chambaux, "Mind your own damn business."

Punishment was swift. The silver handle of a parasol clubbed him hard on the ear. "Sirrah, you will release this woman immediately!"

Clutching his head, he let go of me, whirling to face the duke's mother, the Duchesse de Chambaux. She stood about two feet away, as straight and implacable as a lamppost, wearing a dress in a navy so dark that almost appeared black. A cream lace trimmed the cuff and neck, and a winter bonnet of matching fabric framed the face of this warrior crone.

Next to her stood her daughter, Lady Valentina Fontaine, in a dark rose velvet traveling outfit. Her eyes were wary, her mouth closed tightly, showing that the lines in her face were already settling into the same pattern as her dame's.

Beside them stood three men wearing the coats and flat-brimmed hats of train officials, and around us all was a crowd eager to watch the show.

"I am the Duchesse de Chambaux. Answer your betters, mysir." Her words dripped with contempt, making me almost feel sorry for Buckard. This battle he would not win.

He gave her a sharp nod, seemingly almost against his will, finally acknowledging her higher station. "Duchesse, I am Lord Jansen Buckard."

"I know who you are," she said in a tone that implied he was akin to what pedestrians accidentally stepped in when crossing a dirty street. "I asked what you were doing with this woman. Answer me!" The point of her parasol whacked into the pavement to underscore her words.

"I caught her picking my pocket—"

"You may have told such fairy stories to your doting nurse, Lord Buckard, but do not insult my intelligence. This woman would not be picking pockets, least of all yours. My daughter and I have observed you from the moment you left the train. Have we not, Valentina?"

"Yes, Mother," agreed her daughter dutifully.

"I knew when I recognized you, Lord Buckard, that you could not be trusted to walk across a train platform without causing someone to lament your birth."

"A misunderstanding only. I thought her someone whom I was to meet," insisted Buckard, trying desperately to work his charm, casting about for something that would appease her. He shot an appeal to the railroad men, none of whom seemed disposed to advocate for him.

"Not a pickpocket, but now someone you were meeting? I pity your companions, Lord Buckard. As a woman, I cannot allow you to treat another of my sex with violence under my very nose without intervening. Valentina, take her to our private carriage and let me deal with this person."

Taking the handle of the bag I had dropped when Buckard had

grabbed me, I left with Archambeau's sister. Behind us, he continued digging his grave. "Why bother yourself with such? She is nothing but some low-born—"

"Stop, before you say something that forces me to attend a court action against you. As one of the oldest families in Sarnesse, of the great noble line of Chambaux, I would despise being called to testify against you in a sordid case of libel. However, I know my duty as a woman and a citizen. There are standards we all must meet, Lord Buckard, even if you have forgotten them living your debauched lifestyle."

We reached the black carriage with the Chambaux coat of arms, and the driver jumped down and helped Lady Valentina in first. When I entered, the hem of my too-long dress got caught in the door, and I felt the hasty seam that Dr. LaRue had stitched give way all the way down my back. Quickly, Lady Valentina snapped down the shades on the window.

"I have a change of clothes in my bag, if you can help me?" I asked her.

In silence, she did so.

I changed quickly, so I was wearing my walking dress of coat and skirt by the time the duchesse arrived. She sat beside her daughter and rapped on the ceiling with the handle of her parasol. The carriage pulled away from the train station.

Looking down her long nose at me, her eyes examined me distastefully. "I did not use your name on the public platform, Madame Chalamet, to save you unpleasantness, but pray, tell me, what have you done with Lady Tulip Langenberg?"

"My companion, Dr. LaRue, has taken her to Lindengaard to be reunited with her guardian, Viscount Melgraeve."

Lady Valentina's gaze traveled between her mother and me. When the duchesse said no more, her daughter explained. "We noticed Lady Langenberg roaming the carriage aisle and wondered why she was alone, but had no chance to speak with her."

"And you rescued me, thinking I was Lady Langenberg?" The

duchesse had ridden to the rescue of Lady Tulip and ended up being stuck with a cheap imitation. "Thank you. I needed saving."

The duchesse's gloved fingers did a devil's tap on the handle of her parasol. When her close-set eyes looked down her beaky nose, they gave her a cross look.

"Lord Buckard has a reputation."

Lady Valentina added, in case I did not fully comprehend her mother's meaning, "Not the type of man we would welcome at Hartwood House."

"Lord Buckard is a dangerous man to cross. He will not forget this insulting encounter, Madame Chalamet. My position protects me, but you?" The duchesse grimaced as if my lack of nobility tasted bad. "I recommend you be careful, for he is a vindictive roué."

Chapter Five

When I stepped out of the duchesse's carriage, the sun was setting, casting an orange and violet glow across the heavens. So while it was winter, the first impression I received when viewing the beautiful Lindengaard estate was that everything was cast in golden warmth. Terracotta tiles on the roof, green shutters on every window, and the arched stone entrance felt like an embrace welcoming me home.

Down the drive, narrow columns of green cypress lined the drive like obedient soldiers, and in the distance, the gently rolling hills displayed walled gardens and, further on the horizon, vineyards. It all looked like a painting: the country villa of a country lord.

Servants rushed forward, eager to take our bags. The coach was quickly unloaded, and I gave a silent prayer, hoping my wayward luggage from the train station would make its arrival without mishap.

"Lord Westergaard," said the duchesse to a man I had mistaken for a butler. He air-kissed her hand before giving Lady Fontaine the same courtesy. His bow was effusive but not scraping.

"Welcome to my humble estate. Though I know it cannot

compare to your own beautiful Chambaux, I hope you find yourself comfortable and charmed by it."

He looked like he should have been the lord's librarian: rounded shoulders, probably from hours of desk work, salt-and-pepper hair that had a few unruly curls over his ears, and pale blue eyes that watered easily. His black coat was a little shiny at the cuff and elbows where it had become worn, and he wore no rings, just pewter cufflinks marked with his coat of arms.

Count Westergaard adjusted his thin gold wire spectacles and peered through them, trying to place who I was. When no introduction came from the duchesse or her daughter, he cast me one last look before rushing after the ladies who were already entering the double doors under the front portico.

I took my time in following. Best to break away from the Chambaux family and cut the connection. In my work, I had some dealings with nobility but that was on a business footing; trying to navigate their social circle would be tiresome and probably mean facing down cutting remarks, something I didn't want to do on a holiday excursion.

Grabbing the valise out of the carriage, I entered Lindengaard on my own. Inside, the foyer I found a chaotic scene. We must have arrived right behind a wave of other guests for two dozen or more were all trying to get a servant's attention.

I knew that the Winter Revels always arranged to have the high and low of society attend as a public show of equality. However, while the high were selected due to their connections, and merchants who had a mercantile connection with the royal house invited, the rest were chosen by lottery. Of course, I had used my one noble connection to wrangle my invitation.

From the accents and dress, it seemed all classes were represented, even if there were a few more nobles than merchants and tradespeople.

The first thing I noticed was a fireplace centrally located in the room. Moving over to it, I turned my back to it, placing my hands behind me, to warm them as I took in the scene.

The floor was composed of large blocks of cream gray limestone, scarred in some places with the chisel marks of when it had been quarried. Where we stood had the height of two stories. Stairs on opposite ends of the hall went up to a second story gallery supported by thick ceiling beams that showed the age of the place.

The lime plastered walls were decorated with hunting lodge items: decorative shields emblazoned with coats of arms from days past, spears for boar hunts, animal heads with horns, and even a rather mangy looking bear's head that was missing one of his glass eyes.

Someone elbowed me by accident, apologized, as they rushed past me carrying a valise to follow a servant up one of the staircases. About half an hour later, the group had thinned enough that I finally presented my invitation and got directions to my room.

When I reached our suite, I found Charlotte alone, sitting in a chair, reading a scientific tome about the circulation of the blood.

"Where's Lady Langenberg?"

Charlotte closed her medical volume, giving me her full attention. "She's slipped away to her room. How did things go with Buckard?"

"Handsome as a devil, and as brutish. Like I guessed, he chased after the dress, but wasn't too pleased when he discovered who was wearing it."

I collapsed into another chair beside the doctor's. The room dripped with signs of Old Wealth; the emphasis on old, as the springs in my chair sagged a trifle. Decorated in dark, rather somber colors, it was a fashion out of date by at least two decades, maybe three.

"Anyway, guess who saved me? The Duchesse de Chambaux! She gave Buckard a public tongue lashing, while I beat a retreat."

"The Duchesse? The Duke de Archambeau's mother? I thought she couldn't stand you?"

"Like Buckard, she thought I was Lady Tulip at first, and rushed to rescue her from a cad. Seems it's well known that he's a bad'un. She told him off, and later gave me a warning to watch my back."

"Doesn't sound good for our Tulip," mused Charlotte.

"I agree. We shall have to help her."

"Aren't we here for pleasure?"

"You don't have to help," I said, a little peeved.

Charlotte only shrugged. "I didn't mean I wouldn't help. Just nobility and all that. Damsels in distress. Not my area of expertise."

"We need to know the lay of the land before making a battle plan. Speaking of which, isn't this room a bit on the dowdy side? A bit inconvenient too, being on the third floor, far from the stairs? This looks one step away from being servant quarters." An edge of the wallpaper was peeling up from a corner, and I reached over and flicked it.

"Noticed that, did you? I asked the maid who brought us up. She said ours was the last invitation sent out, and this was the only room Count Westergaard had left to offer. The place is full up and bursting at the seams with lords, ladies, and their servants. They've even converted the barns in the back to house the kitchens and the servants for the competition."

"How much do you want to bet that the hot water is lukewarm by the time it reaches our taps?"

"Bath? There's a shared one down the hall. We have a washbasin."

I groaned. "Not quite the luxury I imagined."

"Cheer up, Elinor. We are in the wing where King Guénard is situated. His party has the entire level, just one floor below us. Don't you feel blessed by his royal presence?"

"I'd much rather eat! I'm starving."

"Now that's what I've been waiting for. Hurry and clean your face. There's a meet-and-greet down in the ballroom. Food and wine. Tables set up by the six chefs that are competing."

She tossed me the program to read for myself as there was a knock at the door. It was staff bringing our trunks from the train station.

"I bet I can get ready before you, Elinor. That's the benefit of trousers."

Downstairs, there was quite the crowd in the ballroom. Crystal chandeliers, reflected in tarnished silver mirrors on the walls, lit it brilliantly. The parquet floor was stained a light chestnut and polished to a reflective gleam. Evergreen shrubs in urns lined the walls, their deep green against the cream-colored plastered walls offering a lovely contrast.

As we entered the hall, a man handed us programs and a little pencil hung on a ribbon we could tie around our wrist. "There is no official judging tonight, but you can use this to write your initial impressions as you visit each of the six tables where a chef will provide food samples. Each table will also have a variety of wines from Count Westergaard's vineyards for you to sample and enjoy."

He didn't have time to tell us more, as another group behind us pushed forward, eager to gain their own programs.

"Where do we start?" Charlotte asked. I pointed my pencil to the right.

Each station had trays of bite-sized samples. After trying some of the offerings, I had to admit that the competition was going to be stiff, for all the food was delicious.

With the lines, it took us an hour to make our way to the table hosted by Chef Perdersen of the Crown. Gerhard, however, was far too busy answering questions from the crowd around his table to have a discussion with me. I didn't want to interfere with him making connections, so just gave him a little wave and smile before tasting the tidbit on a plate handed to me by the server.

"Oh, this is good too," said Charlotte, picking up a second sample.

"I think we are supposed to take only one."

"I'm sure they can make more. I'm starving," was her reply. With her mouth full, she asked, "Recognize anyone? Have you found your pet duke yet? What about his mother?"

"Neither. However, I am intrigued by that lady in black."

She swiveled her gaze to where I pointed, my finger concealed from others by the way I was holding my plate. Charlotte said critically, "Obviously in mourning. At her age, do you think it's a husband or a child?"

"I'm going over to speak with her, so I will let you know."

"Already setting up business, huh? Well, it's your funeral," said my companion. "I've got three more tables to visit. Enjoy yourself."

I made my way through the crowd to the corner of the room, where a lady wearing the deepest mourning sat. Her black satin dress entirely concealed her shoulders and neck, and upon her bosom lay a necklace of jet. The mourning brooch on her shoulder held a lock of hair.

"May I take this seat?"

"I won't stop you."

"Would you like me to get you a refreshment?"

"No."

From afar, I saw Charlotte shake her head and roll her eyes before melting away into the crowd. "Are you here by yourself?"

"No. My son is about somewhere, amusing himself."

I sipped a little from my crystal flute and waited. It didn't take long. She had a story to tell and was looking for an audience. "My Harry would have celebrated his fifty-six birthday this year."

"Was Harry your husband?"

"Yes." She held a handkerchief to her nose and gave a muffled sob, but I noted there was no glint of tears in her eyes. She was putting on a show. It intrigued me. "Harry was always solicitous of me. Home to dinner every evening, tickets to the theater to see my favorites, restaurant reservations, flowers. Nothing was too good for me. But my son? He doesn't care. He even forgot my thirtieth wedding anniversary last month."

"It sounds like your husband loved you very much."

"He did," she said. Her tone of voice piqued my interest even more.

"I see you found a new friend to talk with," said a man, joining us where we sat side by side.

"My son, Herkel Marson," said the widow, giving introductions.

I held out my hand, and he clasped it lightly. "Elinor Chalamet."

His green-brown eyes widened, showing off long black eyelashes in a thin face with an enormous mustache waxed to perfection. He wore the traditional evening dress for a man: black tails and trousers, with a white vest.

"The Ghost Talker of Alenbonné?"

"I see my reputation precedes me."

He shot a sideways look of concern towards his mother before struggling to put on a pleasant smile. "You were mentioned to me by a Mysir Parnell Lafayette."

I gave a light laugh. "Well, I hope you didn't believe all that he said of me? We aren't exactly friendly to each other."

Like most people unused to bluntness, my comment caused him to be silent for a moment. He opened his mouth as if to reply, closed it, and then politely changed the subject. "I hope my mother wasn't bothering you?"

"Oh no. I was getting tired and wanted to be off my feet. It's quite a push tonight, isn't it? I wasn't expecting such a crowd."

"Is this your first time attending the Winter Revels?"

"Yes, is it so obvious?"

His smile grew more sincere. "No, but it's always a crazy rush the first night. I've been to several of them, and it seems that no matter who the host is, they always invite the locals to take part on the first night in order to make the event look bigger than it is. I imagine that once the dinners start, things will calm down, as they are only for the king's guests."

Mysir Marson was too polite to inquire if I was one such, so I volunteered it. "I'm looking forward to it. It will be exciting to see what Chef Perdersen concocts for us to enjoy."

His eyes gleamed with interest, and I sensed a fellow lover of fine food. "Being from Alenbonné, perhaps it isn't a surprise you are backing the chef from the Crown. But I fear he has stiff competition from the Royal Hotel."

His mother had had enough of being ignored. "Herkel, I demand that you take me to my rooms. I feel a headache coming on."

As a dutiful son, he extended his arm to his mother, and she rose to take it. Turning to me, she gave me a stiff goodbye before leaving.

The ghost of her husband, who had been standing behind her chair, gave me a pleading look.

"Help me."

Chapter Six

King Guénard was everywhere, greeting guests with Count Westergaard at his elbow. At one point he even shook Dr. LaRue's hand before moving on to another group, this one containing Lady Tulip Langenberg, who appeared to be avoiding me. By her side was an older gentleman whom I guessed to be her guardian, Viscount Klass Melgraeve.

"Enjoying yourself?"

The Duke de Archambeau startled me. My glass would have spilled if I had not long finished its contents. He deftly took it from my hand and replaced it with a fresh one.

Compared to Buckard's beauty, the duke couldn't compete; his jaw was too square, and his cheekbones too broad. However, while Buckard might make ladies swoon, Archambeau had strength in his features, and it made a woman catch her breath all the same.

"Thank you for the invitations."

Instead of looking pleased at my comment, his eyes narrowed with suspicion. "The only reason for that satisfied expression on your face is because you have found a ghost, or some hapless idiot being possessed. Your nose is positively quivering."

"That makes me sound like a ferret. Not much of a compliment."

"You and I don't traffic in that type of drivel, Chalamet. You know I respect you."

That didn't stop a girl from wanting a few compliments now and then, though.

"It wouldn't be surprising if there were ghosts here, though, would it? If the décor is any indication, Lindengaard must be hundreds of years old."

He took a sip of wine, his eyes scanning the crowd as if he was examining them one-by-one against some invisible checklist in his head. "If you listened to one of the count's long lectures about his family tree, you would think it's been here before Sarnesse was a country, but in fact the grounds have been an estate only for about six hundred years, if you count the first farmhouse on the property. His family took possession of the place about three hundred years ago."

"It doesn't look like a farmhouse to me."

He gave that slight smile. "There are farmhouses for shepherds, and then there are farmhouses for lords. The Westergaards demolished the original and built the villa."

"I imagine your Chambaux estate puts this one to shame."

His gaze locked on someone behind me. He moved abruptly, bending his head to mine. "It appears your friend is seeking you. I shall abscond before I get stabbed, or worse."

The duke bowed before leaving, and a moment later, Charlotte made it to my side.

Before she could say anything about Archambeau, I asked, "What did you think of our king?"

"Needs less food and more exercise," was her verdict.

"Not impressed?"

"No. I'm done with mingling. How about you?"

"I'm ready for bed."

Charlotte swooped in and grabbed two empty glasses and a half-empty bottle of wine on a table which was stacked with discarded napkins and plates. "Let's abscond with our spoils."

―

The next day's weather did not disappoint. There was nothing on the program until that evening, and we were all encouraged to visit the market town of Vouvant for the day. Outside, a line of carriages in the drive were ready to transport anyone who, through delicacy or laziness, would not take the country walk to Vouvant.

Charlotte and I opted for exercise, but before we got very far along the cypress-lined drive, a hail from behind stopped us.

"Madame Chalamet!" It was the widow's son from last night, but his mother was not with him. We paused and let him catch up with us. "How are you today?"

"Fine, thank you. Let me introduce you to my friend, Dr. Charlotte LaRue. Dr. LaRue, Mysir Herkel Marson."

"Are you walking into town? I was wondering if I may have a chat with you? But I don't want to disarrange your plans."

"Our only plan is to enjoy the sunshine," I replied.

We continued on our way, now with Mysir Marson between us. It seemed he had something to confide, and he began in a rush. "I wanted to talk with you about my mother."

"I thought you might. She mentioned losing your father. How long ago did he pass away?"

"He died in a traffic accident about six years ago, and that is the problem. My mother hasn't been the same since his death. I had hoped time would assuage her grief, but she refuses to let go of her mourning. It was because of that I sought help from the Morpheus Society."

"Ah. With Mysir Lafayette?"

"He came highly recommended."

"I'm sure he did." I had put a rooster in Parnell's bed during a conference the last year of my apprenticeship. In return he protested my certification as a Ghost Talker, but he failed. Now, he had far more power in the Morpheus Society and had been circling me for the last two years, looking for a weakness he could exploit.

Mysir Marson continued. "I apologize for her cold dismissal of you last night, but it is because of Mysir Lafayette that she behaved so poorly. Lafayette insisted that my father's spirit had been summoned successfully, but neither of us could see him. And even though he told us things that only my father would know, my mother believed it to be only a trick, playing upon her feelings. It all ended in a dreadful row and with nothing resolved."

I asked, "Is your father a stout man wearing mutton-chop whiskers popular a decade ago, with a slight baldness at the back of his head?"

"That is him to the life! But how would you know this?"

"I saw Harry Marson standing behind your mother during our chat last night. You've done Mysir Lafayette a disservice, for he has brought your father back from the Beyond, and now his ghost is tied to your mother."

Charlotte exclaimed. "Not fair, Elinor. You didn't mention that you saw a ghost to me last night."

My revelation discomfited Marson, and he protested. "But if he did, why can't I see my father? And my mother surely would have a feeling that he was present."

"If you couldn't see him with the aid of Mysir Lafayette, my guess is that you and your mother are psychically blind. Think of it as being color-blind. Only a few can see ghosts unaided, and even with expert assistance, there are some who simply cannot do so."

"I've always seen them when you worked with my cadavers," said Charlotte, a bit smugly.

The mention of corpses startled Mysir Marson, so I was quick to reassure him. "Dr. LaRue is in charge of the Alenbonné morgue. We both work with the gendarmes to solve crimes in our various ways."

He tugged at an earlobe, flustered. "Yes, I think Madame Leona Granger mentioned that when she told me about you. She thought you might have more success with our problem."

"Oh, Madame Granger is my old mentor when I was in training. I would have thought she would have supported Lafayette's findings—"

He admitted reluctantly, "She did, but my mother had taken Ghost Talkers into dislike and refused to listen. My mother has turned away from all her old friends and pleasures. She seems to revel in punishing herself."

"She's getting pleasure from the drama," was Charlotte's judgment, but I rather sensed a mystery here. Guilt seemed more the reason. Guilt about what?

We walked a few more yards before he asked in a defeated tone, "How can I help my mother gain peace of mind if she can't see my father? She seems to need reassurance that he is not in pain, and talks about being forgiven by him. Over what, I do not know."

"Let's take the problem one step at a time. Tonight, make sure you sit beside us at dinner, and we shall discuss what can be done."

Reassured, but still doubtful, he said, "Thank you, Madame Chalamet. I will do anything you ask." Tipping his hat, he excused himself with an "Until tonight, ladies."

When he was out of earshot, Charlotte poked me in the ribs. "Now tell me everything you didn't want to tell sonny!"

I chuckled. "I've said all I know."

"Never!" insisted my friend. "I know that look on your face all too well."

"You're the second person to say my face gives me away! Anyway, it's just guesswork for now, and I could be wrong. But there are two reasons for ghosts, my friend. One, the ghost has unfinished business. And two, the living won't release them.

Considering what Marson said, I would guess his wife is holding Harry here."

"I don't see that it helps. The woman denies his presence."

"While I don't like it, sometimes you must stoop to using tricks in order to convince the most stubborn of the truth."

"Well, don't feel too bad about it, Elinor; I've prescribed a sugar pill or two myself."

By this time we had reached the town center, which was bustling with Winter Revel attendees going in and out of the town shops. The houses of pink stucco and tan bricks, the black-and-white-striped shop awnings, and freshly painted signs that declared where you could find bonnets or yarn, all made a charming picture.

It all looked manicured and immaculate. Stage-managed to perfection. However, considering the number of packages coming out of the stores in the hands of visitors, perhaps Vouvant had invested into itself wisely.

I stopped in front of the Royal Bank. "I have some business to attend to, if you don't mind, Charlotte?"

"Go ahead."

There was a small line in the bank, but it moved quickly. Sliding some notes to the teller, I gave her my instructions and was back out on the pavement within twenty minutes.

Charlotte bent her head close to mine and said quietly, "Saw that Buckard fellow. Or someone who matched that description: handsome, arrogant, and ugly eyes. He followed our Tulip into that shop across the road."

"Hm. Perhaps it's time to engage with the enemy."

We made our way across the street. Peering into the shop window, I saw the wickedly handsome Lord Jansen Buckard had cornered Lady Tulip Langenberg. Literally. He had backed her against the wall, her hands captured in his, while he whispered some foulness in her ear, if the horrible look on her face was any indication.

The shopkeeper was helping an older couple, one of whom was the man who had been with Lady Tulip at last night's festivities. They seemed engrossed in selecting pastries from the display case, unaware of the drama playing out between the young girl and the aristo.

No! I saw the man's eyes shift towards Lady Tulip before returning to the acquisition of cream puffs. He knew what was happening and was doing absolutely nothing to protect her.

"Follow my lead, all right?" I said, and Charlotte nodded.

The bell rang as I opened the bakery door, but no one looked our way. Besides the well-dressed older couple, Lady Tulip, and Lord Buckard, there were two young girls wearing cheaply ruffled dresses in bright, garish colors. Garish clothes could be interpreted as a link to a credulous nature: the woman wanted to believe that extra layers of flounces, lace, and ribbons made her beautiful. Add a hairstyle with an abundance of tight, artificial curls, a child-like, vacant stare, and a rosebud mouth, and I couldn't have asked for a better volunteer for the plan forming in my head.

My eyes immediately fastened upon a piece of mourning jewelry: a brooch with a lock of light-colored hair on the breast of one girl. There was always one in the crowd, someone devoted to seeing ghosts and ready to believe.

"This is the place!"

My loud statement drew everyone's stares.

I put my hands up in the air and vibrated my fingers above my hand, closing my eyes. "Can you feel it in the air, doctor?"

Charlotte looked around, squinting speculatively at the ceiling. "Now that you mention it, I do, Madame Ghost Talker. Do you think the spirits will speak?"

I have very keen hearing. The two young girls muttered excitedly to each other, giving me a name. While I wished being an honest Ghost Talker was enough to do my trade, resorting to stage tricks often aided the work. I tried to soothe my conscience by never taking money in such cases.

"Is there someone here named Cynthia?" I asked loudly. The one wearing the brooch gasped and raised her hand shyly. I reached out my hand, beckoning to her. "Come, do not be afraid. I am Madame Chalamet, a medium, and there is a spirit here who wishes to communicate with you."

She glanced around the room, hardly believing it was her I wanted, before stepping slowly over to me. "I lost my little brother when we were children. It must be him!"

"Tell me no more, my dear." Facing her, I took her hands in my own. My thumbs started stroking her wrists, feeling the jump of her pulse. There is a form of control that one person can exert over another if they are susceptible, and Mistress Cynthia was more than willing to be led. Like an obedient horse, her pulse quickly matched its rhythm to my stroking request.

"His name starts with a B—" She didn't blink. I tried again, mentally skimming through the most popular male names of ten years ago. "V— yes, Vernon?"

She gasped again and started nodding. Really, it was far too easy to play this game. No wonder folk like Madame Nyght took to deception like a duck to water.

"A little boy with flaxen curls?"

You could see the gulp in her throat. "Yes—"

"Quiet, child. Relax. I am here to help you." I stroked her forehead, drawing my hands down to either side of her face. They served as blinders, directing her gaze only forward to my own. Her lips parted. "Yes, Vernon has something he wishes to convey to you."

As Lord Buckard recognized me, his face contorted with barely controlled fury. However, the ladies in the room were holding their breath, waiting for the drama to unfold. Women know about loss, and gaining a message from Beyond is not only fascinating, but confirms that those we love continue after they leave us. We all need that reassurance, even I.

"He had a favorite toy—"

The girl murmured, "A toy soldier—"

"Painted in red and black." She was swaying, mesmerized by my gaze and voice. I saw her pupils dilate as she leaned towards me, her body growing compliant under my stronger will.

"Yes, my dear, he has a message of love and forgiveness for you. He forgives you. And your family. No one is at fault for his death."

The girl gave a low moan and swooned.

I cried out, "Catch her!"

Chapter Seven

Trained from childhood, even a blackguard like Lord Buckard could not let a woman hit the floor. Panther-like, he sprang and seized the fainting girl.

"Put her in this chair here," I commanded him. He did as I asked while Lady Tulip, free from him, hastened to her guardian's side.

After settling the girl as best he could, Buckard glared at me with hearty dislike. "You did this, witch."

"Oh, not a witch, Lord Buckard, only a Ghost Talker. Now, if you will step away, I shall take care of her."

The girl's companion was beside her, fanning the face of her fallen friend. "What's wrong with her?" She glanced up at Charlotte. "Your friend called you a doctor?"

"Yes, I am a doctor," said Charlotte, as she took up the unconscious girl's wrist to feel a pulse. "She's fine. It's strong."

"No need to be alarmed," I explained to the girl's friend. "Your friend is in a deep sleep, a trance, and I will wake her up in just a moment. But now, your name, please?"

"I am Melody Cantrell, Cynthia's cousin."

"Mys Cantrell, what is the circumstance of her brother's death? Do you know of it?"

"Yes," she said hesitantly, looking around the room at all the interested faces.

"Do not concern yourself with them. None will speak of this matter, will they?"

Everyone nodded their reassurance, though I was relatively certain they would all gossip about it later no matter their promises.

Cynthia said in a quiet voice, "Her little brother drowned at the lake where the family was picnicking. He stole away, and they found him later in deep water near the boat dock. It a great tragedy for her family."

"Thank you for your help." Bringing a stool to where the girl slumped unconscious on the bench, I bent close to examine her.

Her extreme response might seem spectacular to an outsider, but anyone trained by the Morpheus Society knew how susceptible human nature was to a more powerful personality. She was clay, and I was the artist. Now it was time to shape her into something stronger and better.

Talking in a low voice, I began. "Cynthia, let us go back in time. With every number I say, you will go back one year."

On the number nine, the girl's eyes moved rapidly under their lids, disturbed.

"It is summer. Feel the warmth of the sun on your skin? The playful breeze on your cheek? In the distance, you see the light on the water. You are at the lake with your parents. Your brother is there."

She stirred, her brow creasing. She murmured, "No. I don't want to go there."

I took her limp hand in my own, holding it gently. "I am with you. You are safe. This is just an old picture— a daguerreotype. Nothing can hurt you by looking at a picture. Look at the picture and tell us, what is your brother doing?"

"He wants my ball."

"A beautiful ball. So pretty. And he wants your ball," I repeated.

"Yes. Mummy gave it to me, not him. He always wants what I have." Her voice had grown younger, more childish in tone.

"You are playing with the ball."

"Tossing it so high he can't reach it."

"Tossing the ball. High. Higher. Then you threw the ball where he would never get it."

"Serves him right. Papa always gives him the better toys! He should play with his soldiers!"

"You threw the ball so far. Far, far away, so he would never, ever get it. But he still wanted it, didn't he, Cynthia? And he went after it."

"I didn't know. Didn't know—" A tear slid out of her lashes and went down the curve of her cheek. She gave a hiccup of a sob in the quiet shop. Even Lord Buckard had stopped muttering under his breath to listen.

"It's all right, Cynthia. You didn't know Vernon would go after the ball in the water. I know. Vernon knows. He's here now and wishes to speak to you."

"He does?" Wonder and disbelief colored her voice.

"Don't you see him? Standing near that tree?"

"Oh, yes. Vernon!"

"Hand him the ball, Cynthia. You want him to have the ball now."

"Vernon, please take it! I want you to have it." After a moment, her voice grew warmer. "He took it! He looks so happy."

"See, Vernon knows you love him. That you want to be his friend."

She sighed again.

To her cousin, I said in a low voice, "Get a glass of juice if they have something at the counter. She'll need a restorative when she wakes." Turning back, I addressed the entranced girl. "Now it's time for Vernon to leave."

"No! I want him to stay and be my friend."

"Vernon must go to a place you cannot. See that black ribbon tied around your wrist? See how it ties you to your brother? It's too tight."

She jerked her hand out of mine and swatted at her other wrist. "Make it go away! It hurts!"

"It is going away. You will pull the ribbon's tie and it will slide off. Watch. Three—two—one. The ribbon has fallen. It is on the ground."

"It is!"

"Look at your brother. Vernon's ribbon is gone as well."

"He's so happy."

"Good. Now it's time to say goodbye. You are letting him go."

"Bye-bye, Vernon," she said in her child's voice.

I cricked my neck to the right and to the left, popping a joint.

"Ten—nine—eight— you are walking away from the lake. It is fading away to a memory. A good memory of how you loved your brother. You remember only love. Seven—six— you are coming back to us, to your cousin Melody, who loves you. Five—four— you are lighter now, all is falling away, as you come back to today. The picnic at the lake feels long ago. The memory of that day is fading like an old picture. Three—two—and one. You are at peace. Now, open your eyes."

Mys Cynthia's eyelashes fluttered, and she blinked, dazed. I extended my hand, and her cousin gave me a small glass of chilled orange juice.

"It was so stuffy in here, Mys Cynthia, that you fainted. Here, sip this and take a moment to recover."

Obediently, she took the glass from my hand. To Mys Melody, I said, "She should be fine, but I suggest taking her home for a rest. Or if she feels energetic, do a short walk around the plaza. Healing affects everyone differently, but keep an eye on her over the next few days. If you need me, you will find me at Lindengaard during the Winter Revels."

Melody Cantrell asked, "But what did you do? What happened to her?"

"Sometimes we hold on to things that do not serve us well. She released her guilt about her brother's accident." I stressed the last word.

Cynthia seemed unaware of our conversation. Handing her empty glass to the girl at the counter, she smoothed down her dress. "We are going to be late, Melody, if we don't hurry."

Melody agreed. The two girls quickly left, and the shop returned to normal. Lord Buckard tipped his hat to Lady Tulip and her guardian, bidding them a polite goodbye before exiting. Lady Tulip and her family turned away, picking up the parcels wrapped in pink ribbons that held their selections. Lady Tulip's cheeks were alabaster and her frozen gaze stared ahead, not meeting our silent inquiry as she passed us.

Well, good deeds often went unrewarded.

Surveying the pastry display case, I asked, "Charlotte, isn't it time for a little something?"

When we returned to our rooms, on each of our pillows was a folded card. Opening it, we found the elaborate menu for the evening.

Tonight's round was between two chefs, Beinhouwer and Chapelle, both of whom were in private service. Their first course was to be dueling cream soups: a bisque of shrimp, and another of artichokes. The next course was fish, bluefish versus halibut, followed by glazed ham versus veal, and lastly squab versus lamb. The sides included a cold salad and vegetables: cauliflower, asparagus, potatoes, and carrots. Desserts were to be announced.

"What do you think? Who will win?" asked Charlotte.

"I have eaten nothing by either of these chefs, and this is a very bare description. Who will win tonight depends on taste and preparation. That you don't find on a menu card."

Charlotte used the washstand and patted her face and hands dry with a towel. She was obsessive about washing her hands and when finished, always lathered them with lotion. She asked curiously, "By the way, how did you know all those details about that girl?"

"Experience and deduction."

I explained to her that as soon as we had entered the bakery, I'd noticed that Cynthia wore a Death Remembered jet brooch encasing a curly strand of blond hair. A memento like that was commonly worn by those who had lost someone close to them, such as a spouse, parent or a sibling. Last night, Madame Marson had also worn such a piece of jewelry.

"At her age, it was easy to deduce it was a sibling or parent. I used popular male baby names at the time her brother was likely to be born. She gave me the rest."

"It sounds more like trickery than communing with ghosts. Didn't you learn anything from the little boy, her brother?"

"No. I couldn't summon him, which means he probably has transitioned to the Afterlife despite the tragedy. I had to find other ways to help his sister give up her guilt about her part in his death."

Charlotte pressed, "But the ball she threw into the water? How did you know that happened, or that she felt guilty about it, without talking to her brother?"

"When a loved one dies, there is always guilt of some kind the living holds on to. Could they have prevented the tragedy? Should they have called the doctor sooner? If they only hadn't left the window open, the lamp lit, or decided not to picnic at the lake. The 'had I but known' regret is very common. Time usually wears that away, but in Cynthia's case, she was still holding on to those feelings."

She shook her head. "No matter how many times I see you work with people, I don't understand how you figure out their lives or what they need. Are human souls that easy? I've never found them to be so."

"People and their problems interest me. I think *you* like those that can't talk back. Now, enough of that. What are you wearing tonight?"

Without Anne-Marie, it was up to us to dress and style ourselves. Looking at my reflection in the mirror when she had finished, Charlotte grimaced at what she had achieved with my hair. "I'm not very good at this."

"Don't worry. I'm not here for fashion, but for food. You sit down and see how well I do."

Slicking her hair back on the sides with my brush, I brought her shoulder-length dark hair into a small bun at the base of her neck. From my jewelry box, I selected a pair of ruby earrings that I had brought especially for her. She opened her mouth to protest, but I stopped her.

"Merely a loan. These will look stunning on you, and I insist. I'm glad you have your ears pierced, despite never wearing anything in them."

With the angular features of her face, she may not have been beautiful, but she was definitely striking. She was always a woman to be noticed, but this time I felt it would be more than her trousers and lack of societal manners that would draw attention.

We had just a few last-minute details to take care of. Standing in front of the mirror, I adjusted my neckline once again. It still didn't quite cover the mark under my collarbone, almost over my heart. With women's fashion dictating that evening wear was off the shoulders, I draped a light scarf around my shoulders and pinned it to the bodice, concealing the crescent-shaped burn left by my father's watch.

Dr. LaRue wore a gentleman's black tail coat, but the trousers had a wide leg, swinging around her ankles. Instead of a white cravat, she tied one of emerald green with a pattern of tiny circles in yellow around her neck.

"Ready?"

She held out her arm, and together we left to make our way to the dining hall for the first of the four Winter Revel dinners.

Chapter Eight

Entering the ballroom, we found it set up with banquet tables. They gave Charlotte and I different tables; guests were being separated to promote conversation and to ensure fair judging.

King Guénard was at the head table, which seated six, along with Count Westergaard and a few other dignitaries I didn't recognize. This table faced the other four that seated twelve, making the Winter Revel's diners total fifty-four.

Archambeau was at Charlotte's table, along with Viscount Melgraeve, Lady Tulip's guardian. The duke's mother and sister were at another, but seated at opposite ends. Lady Tulip Langenberg was at my table, though too far away to share a discussion; I did not see Lord Buckard, for which I was thankful.

"Madame Chalamet."

"Mysir Marson."

He pulled out my seat and then took his own next to mine. "Did you enjoy your visit to Vouvant?" he asked as other diners took their seats.

"I did. It's very picturesque, with all the buildings made from that same pink-gray stone."

"It's from a local quarry close to here."

"Oh, are you a local?"

"No, but I've visited the town before on business. Of course, I wasn't staying at Lindengaard, but in the village." From behind us, the servers poured out wine that, from the label, was from Count Westergaard's vineyard. Mysir Marson gave his glass a speculative sniff. "Are we to judge the wine also, do you think?"

"There isn't a place on the judging card to do so." I showed him the card I had pulled out from under my plate, which gave the list of dishes and a place to score them. "By the way, is it just a lucky chance that we they seated us together?"

"We were at the same table, but I switched cards before the room filled."

So Marson was clever and a quick thinker.

"I noticed your mother's absence from the party. How is she doing?"

"She refused to leave her room." The corners of his mouth hardened with irritation.

"We all grieve in our own way." It was one of those platitudes that was actually true.

"While I would normally agree with you, Madame Chalamet, I have been living with this excessive mourning for several years. It makes for a very uncomfortable life."

From the head table, a bell chimed, signifying a speech. The king rose, welcomed us all, and gave a brief biography of the two chefs who were competing in the first round. I'm afraid I heard little of it, because the first course was coming out of the kitchen and the smells were distracting. Two shallow bowls held the cream soups: one of shrimp, the other artichoke. They arrived side by side for our tasting.

"What are your thoughts, madame?" asked my table companion.

"I do not want to influence your judging—"

"You won't! Rest assured, I have my own mind."

We talked it over, trying to guess the ingredients. Marson was a pleasant enough dinner partner, and knowledgeable about fine cuisine. His comments were thoughtful and polite, but still I found my gaze wandering across the room to where Archambeau sat. What did he think of the dishes? Did he care? Perhaps it was his dinner partner, a woman dressed in gold and black with a ruby necklace around her neck, and not the food that made him appear bored?

"It looks like they are getting ready for the next course," said Mysir Marson.

Hastily, I made a tick and a comment or two using the gold-colored pencil I'd found next to my judging card. For me, it was hard to taste the shrimp in the first soup. It lacked body and smelled strongly fishy, making me wonder how old the shrimp had been. The artichoke, with its creamy blend of subtle flavor, was the clear winner.

The next course was fish. From living in a harbor town, I knew bluefish needed to be bled soon after being caught. I wondered if the chef would have known this?

After the shrimp bisque I feared the worst, but my concerns were for naught. It came broiled, sitting on paper-thin, golden-brown potatoes cooked to perfection and a creamy cold sauce composed of olive oil, egg, and garlic. It smelled wonderful, and the dressing was perfection.

The chefs must be moving quickly in the kitchen, for the halibut, seasoned with pepper, thyme, and lemon, with a side of asparagus, came next. Its delicate texture melted in my mouth. In the end, to me the two fish dishes were both equal, but I gave a slight edge to the bluefish since it was a more difficult dish to prepare correctly.

Around the delivery of our dishes, we discussed the problem of Mysir Marson's mother. "How did you get involved with Mysir Parnell?"

"Mother wanted to pass on a message to my father. To speak

with him. Mostly, though, she seemed to desire reassurance that he was at peace. So he did a séance at our home." Mysir Marson sighed and looked out over the tables as if remembering painful events.

"He insisted he had summoned my father, but neither myself nor Mother could see him. Then Mysir Parnell passed along some information about my father's life that only he and my mother would know. His favorite food, the dressing gown he'd worn before bed. But this information did not reassure her. Instead, it seemed to have the opposite effect that he intended, for my mother became hysterical and shut it all down. She refused to discuss it or to meet again with Mysir Parnell."

Parnell was not known for his diplomacy, and his contempt for women was something of a legend amongst those in the Society. He angered me at the conference, when I had overheard him in the hallway talking with a group of men about a female Ghost Talker who he said was unsuited to the work because she was to emotional being a woman.

The next course arrived, smelling delicious. I took a moment to savor it before saying, "How much do you know about the theory of why some who die become ghosts while others don't, Mysir Marson?"

"Not much. I'm a chemist with a dispensary. While my pharmacy deals with the sick and dying, my job is mostly in compounding what a doctor prescribes. Ghosts never concerned me until my father passed."

"Strong needs create ghosts. When a ghost stays in the Beyond, refusing to cross to the Afterlife, it could be because of unfinished business, a traumatic death, or an attachment to someone. Some powerful emotion, like jealousy or terror, usually ties them to the Earthly plane."

He paused, considering my words, before telling me how his father had died.

"A carriage ran him down when he was on his way to pick up a book my mother had ordered from a local shop. I would have thought he'd haunt the street where it happened, not my mother."

"That is a good point. That is another classification of a haunt — one that is tied by a place, rather than an emotion. We can find those hauntings at places of disaster or historical significance. However, your father's spirit seems very attached to his wife, instead of where he died."

"He was very devoted to her. Waited on her hand and foot. It's probably why she finds fault with everything I do, since I am not as attentive."

The meat course arrived, and we both had to sort out the carving. More wine came by. I would have to swim out of here, or be carried.

"There are two options here. Your father has an Attachment and cannot leave. Or your mother has a Binding."

"What's that?" Marson asked curiously.

"A Binding happens when someone living refuses to let go of the deceased. Their emotional bond is so strong that the soul cannot transition to the Afterlife." In some ways, it was like the problem of the girl in the bakeshop, except hers had been a mental binding upon herself, since her brother had transitioned.

Dessert was very disappointing, hardly worth mentioning. Very weak and pedestrian. If I were to judge from that course alone, both would lose. It was not always a given that a chef who cooked the main meal could also do pastry. I pushed the pudding aside, leaving most on my plate as a server with a basket circled the tables, asking for our menu scores.

"Do you think you can cut this Attachment or Binding?"

"Certainly, I will do my best, Mysir Marson. Tomorrow, if the weather is fine, make sure you and your mother stroll the gardens after lunch. I will find you."

We parted ways soon after rising; Mysir Marson said his

mother would become quarrelsome if he lingered. I watched him go, my mind going over possibilities of what I would do.

"Thinking, Chalamet? That's what gets you into trouble," said Tristan Fontaine, Duke de Archambeau. He had materialized at my elbow, taking Marson's seat.

"Would you rather I not?"

"No. An ornamental role is not for you."

"Now you imply I'm not pretty enough. You really need to brush up on your banter, Your Grace."

Our eyes locked, and I wondered what had caused that little scar on his chin.

"Are you telling me you would rather spend your day browsing fashion plates, writing letters, and practicing your dance steps?"

"Is that what society ladies do?"

"It's what my sister does. And watercolors. She paints a very excellent watercolor. But please do not ask her to play the piano. Despite threats from Mother, she always skipped her practice, and it shows."

His eyes surveyed the room, scanning it, always watching. His gaze hesitated when it found Lady Tulip, and I felt myself blush. Did the man know?

"So, my mother informed me earlier today that you had a misadventure at the train station." He sounded a bit aloof. Were his feelings hurt about something?

"Lady Langenberg needed help. What do you know about her?"

"Her family is a distant branch of the king's. Which isn't surprising, considering how inbred the aristocracy is. She debuted last season and refused all suitors because of her high principles. 'Foolishly idealistic' is how my sister describes her. Men find her lectures on social reform tedious, but listen politely because she comes with a substantial dowry."

"Did she have many suitors?"

"I wouldn't know, Chalamet, I didn't count them," he told me mockingly.

"What about her guardian, Viscount Melgraeve?"

"Man about town. Dabbles in high finance and got burned last year buying speculative stock in a Zulskaya gold mine scheme."

"Oh, I read about that! It was on the front pages of the newssheets for weeks."

Archambeau's face hardened, and his eyes narrowed as if was thinking of skewering someone. "Unfortunately, the Zulskaya government disavows any responsibility for the scam, yet they refuse to extradite the scoundrel so we can dispense Sarnesse justice."

I didn't want to talk about politics, so I asked, "What are your thoughts on Lord Jansen Buckard?"

"Be careful, Chalamet. Buckard has a rabid bite. He's ruined more than one society woman. Hm. I can see by that stubborn expression on your face that you will not be taking my advice."

I said meekly, "Thank you for the tickets."

"Don't play the young mys with me, Chalamet. That won't wash! All these questions about Buckard, Langenberg, and Melgrave mean you are sticking your nose into everyone's business, whether or not they want you to."

Leaning closer, my shawl slipping off my shoulders, I said confidentially, "But people fascinate me. Curiosity about them is my weakness."

Our stares fenced, trying to find a weakness, and then we both dropped our weapons at the same time. His eyes cast down, he said, almost angrily, "How did you hurt yourself? Was it Buckard?"

My hand went up and readjusted the scarf that had fallen, exposing the crescent scar above my heart. "A small thing. Nothing of consequence."

"Here you are," said Dr. LaRue, interrupting us.

Archambeau rose from his chair, giving Charlotte a curt bow. "Ah, the doctor who likes to stick her patients with swords."

"Technically, you were not my patient when I tried to stab you."

"I stand corrected. I think I see the king is requesting my presence. Good evening, ladies." He gave us a bow and left.

Charlotte said with raised eyebrows, "You two seemed cozy. Maybe you could influence the king through your friend, the duke, to help our Tulip?"

"It is a card that I may play, but let us first see what happens."

We stayed for another half an hour, but finding ourselves yawning behind our hands, we retreated to our rooms.

Charlotte handed me the ruby earrings before changing into her nightdress, a very dowdy thing of thick cotton that went to her toes. Slipping under her sheets, the doctor lay on her back, pulling a night mask over her eyes.

"You can sit up if you like, but I'm dead on my feet. Talking to living people is exhausting. And I'm as stuffed as a mid-winter pig."

I took out the pins in my hair and brushed it. I was about to braid it when there was a low knock at our door. Charlotte slipped a finger under her mask and one eye looked inquiringly at me. "Expecting anyone?"

"No, not me. It must be one of your admirers. Perhaps Marson to weep about his dear mother? Or the duke to leer at your bosom again?"

Grabbing a pillow from my bed, I threw it at her head. She ducked under the covers. Belting my robe and cracking open the door, I revealed Lady Tulip Langenberg in the corridor. She was still wearing the deep purple velvet dress from dinner, and draped around her shoulders was a dark, glossy brown fur stole.

"May I come in?"

"Certainly." I stepped back and closed the door behind her.

Seeing Charlotte in bed, she said hurriedly, "I didn't mean to disturb you."

"No worries. We hadn't really gone to sleep yet, despite appearances. Come and sit over here." I invited her over to our two chairs and gave her the one without the broken spring. "Did you enjoy the dinner?"

"Not really. I couldn't eat." In a rush, her face changing from red to white, she said, "Thank you for all of your help— on the train and in the bakery. I don't want you to think I'm not grateful."

"Never worry about that. We didn't think so."

She rushed on, her words racing out of her mouth like a runaway horse. "I just visited King Guénard, and he refused to assist me. He said I should grow up and understand how the world works. Girls get married to whom their elders pick, and afterward, when I've had a child or two, I could pick a companion more genial to me."

Clearly, King Guénard did not know much about how to speak to young ladies with high principles. His jaded statement about marriage and lovers might be what the upper classes did, but it was not the words a young, virginal lady facing her first marriage wanted to hear. We would all like to believe that with intimacy came love and I could not help but feel sympathetic toward Lady Tulip's quandary.

I begged her, "Let me talk to Mysir de Chambaux on your behalf. I'm sure he will help. He's very close with King Guénard and has influence he could use on your behalf."

From her place on her bed, Charlotte said slyly, "Archambeau is a friend of Elinor's."

Tulip's eyes flickered and her words seemed to reflect her inner thoughts, with little thought for her audience. "The king's man? The duke? No. He would not help. Not a man who bowed to convention and made a match for convenience himself. If even someone as powerful as he had to bend, then what hope is there for me?"

She stood up and made her way to the door. Facing it, she said brightly, "Really, don't worry. All will be fine."

Before I could protest or add any reassurance, she was gone.

Chapter Nine

I was dreaming of a séance that had never happened.

Across the table from where I sat, Madame Nyght wore a caftan with a pattern of green palm fronds and orange tigers that prowled across the sleeves, their yellow eyes as bright as lamps.

Nyght had her eyes closed, palms flat down on the table as she crooned. "Come to me, spirits! Come to me!"

"You're a fraud, Madame Nyght!" I shouted at her.

Her eyes snapped open as she countered, "Aren't you? Using my tricks?"

Suddenly, the table under our hands lifted, rising into the air, as the sound of ghostly knocking started. Rap-rap.

Classic table turning.

"Two raps mean a yes," said Madame Nyght.

Rap-rap-rap-rap.

"What do four raps mean?" I demanded.

"Answer the door," said Charlotte, and my eyes popped open.

I struggled out from under my blankets, knocking my pillow to the floor. Putting my arms through my robe, I belted it.

Fully expecting another visit from Lady Tulip, it surprised me to see the Duke de Archambeau instead. He was still wearing his outfit from dinner, but his cravat was gone and the first button on his shirt undone, black chest hairs showing at the base of his exposed throat.

I blinked. Was I still dreaming?

Abruptly, he pushed past me and addressed Charlotte, who was sitting up in bed, her mask off, and her eyes immediately on alert.

"Dr. LaRue, I have a patient who needs you."

Like a hound that hears the hunting horn, Charlotte was immediately alert. She sprang out of bed and pulled a blue robe over her long nightgown. From under the bed, she pulled out her black valise holding her medical gear.

"I'm ready."

"Follow me. Quickly, but discreetly."

It must have been very early in the morning, for we met no one in the hall or on the staircase, not even servants. Archambeau's stride made us trot to keep up as we went down a flight and turned. I had a sick feeling I knew where we were going— to the king's room.

Archambeau gave a sharp double rap, pause, and another rap, and the door opened to reveal a short, very frightened middle-aged man. He quickly ushered us in, stuttering, "Is this the d-d-doctor?"

Inside was a shocking scene. King Guénard lay on a chaise lounge, his body limp and his eyes closed. His skin was pale and sweaty. I could not see if he was breathing. Charlotte was at his side in a flash, checking his pulse. Next, she pulled a stethoscope out of her case and started using it, even as she talked.

"How long since he collapsed?"

When no one answered, Archambeau snapped his fingers in front of the short man's face as if to wake him up. "Simon, answer her. Now!"

Wringing his hands and fluttering about like a moth battering itself to death against a light, Simon said, "About an hour ago. At first he said his stomach was upset."

"Did he vomit?" asked Charlotte.

The man pointed weakly to a bowl resting across the room on the floor. I handed it to her. She pulled on a pair of leather gloves from her case and, using one of her scalpels, started examining it. "How long after the vomiting before he collapsed?"

"A half-hour. Maybe. I guess?"

"Have you done anything for him?" demanded Charlotte.

The duke answered. "Not much. Simon came to my room and when we got back, he was as you see. You are the only physician here that I'm personally acquainted with. And one I trust to keep her mouth shut."

"He's breathing, but it's shallow, and his heart is galloping like a three-legged horse. I need light in here. Elinor, bring that candelabra over here."

She examined his hands, pressing a fingernail deeply into his fingers with no response. Lifting his eyelids, Charlotte examined his pupils one by one. They were bloodshot and unseeing. It was truly unnerving to see the king in such a state.

Using a tongue depressor, the doctor pried open the king's mouth and smelled his breath. Then she examined his tongue, which even to my unpracticed eye looked swollen and a strange color. A prick with a needle gained no reaction.

"Now, what and when did he eat last? Has he had anything to drink in the last few hours?"

Archambeau looked at the king's man, who refused to meet his eyes. In seconds, the duke leapt across the room and grabbed the man by the throat, throwing him against the wall in a burst of violence that left the man's legs dangling helplessly off the floor.

"I don't care about Guénard's gluttony, Simon. What did he eat?! Or are you guilty of more than stupidity? The doctor needs to know. *Now!* Answer her."

The king's aide stumbled over his words, trying to figure out what he could say that would get him into the least amount of trouble. "It was a dessert, sent up by one of the chefs. They've been sending him little treats since we arrived. Just tokens of their favor."

"That was the only thing since dinner?"

"Yes. He said it tasted bad and didn't finish it."

"How long after he ate it did he become ill?" asked Charlotte.

"Maybe half an hour. Or less. I'm not sure." The man was visibly trembling. The duke dropped his grip but snarled. "And where is that little treat now?"

"I'm guessing it was this," I said, pointing at a little table where a cloth napkin partially covered a small plate.

"Don't touch it," warned Charlotte. "I suspect poison at this stage. His tongue shows a caustic burn. Did he have any wine?"

"Only water," gulped the frightened assistant.

Charlotte and Archambeau joined me at the table. With a magnifying lens, she examined the layers she pulled apart with her scalpel. "I need a clean spoon and a blue-glass bottle."

Archambeau snapped his fingers, and Simon rushed about the room, bringing the requested items. Emptying the bottle's contents onto the floor, Charlotte took it by its neck and, and holding her arm over her eyes, smashed it against the corner of the table.

Simon gasped. "That was fifty-year-old brandy! Sent up by Count Westergaard as a gift!"

"Shut up, Simon. I've had enough of these gifts," Archambeau told him.

From the glass, Charlotte took one large piece, the round base, and set it aside. Placing a candle on the table, she took a clean spoon, scraped some white sediment from the dessert that appeared to be sugar, and held it over the candle. In a few moments it flamed, and she held the blue glass up to her eye to examine it.

"Do you smell it?"

"Garlic?" I queried.

"It's as I suspected. Look." She handed the glass to the duke and bade him to look at the flame.

"It looks purple, but without the glass, the flame appears white. I don't understand."

"Exactly. The color of the glass filters out the yellow. A straightforward test to see if certain poisons are present. Arsenic in the food. But he would need to consume quite a bit— and this dessert looks almost untouched. Why would he have such a severe reaction? You," she pointed at Simon, "Do you know anything about the king's health? What he takes? Does he have any chronic conditions? Medication?"

"There is a bottle of powder he uses in the bathroom, but he's taken that for years and never had a problem."

In seconds, Archambeau re-emerged, and gave the doctor an amber-colored medicine bottle. She looked at the label and snorted. "*Dr. Lilly's patented slimming solution for those who want to encourage health.* This slop puts more people on my slab than you realize. Did he have any of this tonight?"

"When we came back from dinner," said Simon.

"How much? It says the dose here is a tablespoon." By Simon's expression, we all knew the king hadn't taken just a tablespoon. "How much?" repeated Charlotte loudly.

"Three tablespoons?" quavered the king's man.

"Can you do anything?" Archambeau demanded.

Charlotte returned to using her stethoscope, pressing it against the king's chest while the room remained deathly quiet. "The acute poisoning is causing myocardial damage. My recommendation is an immediate injection of digitalis. It strengthens the heartbeat, though it could be a risk."

Behind the king's inert form, a pale mist was forming.

"Whatever you are going to do, Charlotte, you need to do it now. The king's soul is leaving his body."

To Archambeau, she asked, "Do I have your permission to proceed? Understanding the cure might kill him?"

"Proceed."

I glanced from the king's clammy face, now tinged with blue, to the duke. Archambeau's face was grim, haggard even. Whatever happened here tonight, he would take the blame, or the accolades, upon his head.

Charlotte worked with cold efficiency. She brought out a vial from her case and prepared the syringe, then started searching for a vein in the king's arm.

"Here we go," she murmured. Nothing happened immediately. Charlotte gave instructions to the king's man. "Get me a slightly warm face cloth, wrung out." To Archambeau she said, "A blanket." She took the stethoscope and listened again. "How's the king's soul, Elinor?"

"About the same."

Taking the washcloth from Simon, she wiped out the inside of the king's mouth, teeth, and lips, and set it aside. "I'd burn that cloth, but save the vomit. I want to run tests on that later. Keep time for me, Your Grace."

He picked up a small clock by the king's bedside while Charlotte loaded her syringe a second time. "If we don't see a result, I'll try again."

Excitedly, I told them, "He's fading! I mean, his soul is fading, Charlotte. He's returning to his body."

Simon cried out. "His eyes are opening!"

"Don't move, Your Majesty. My name is Charlotte LaRue and I'm a doctor. You've just suffered a heart attack." She returned to listening to his heart while we held our breath. In a few moments, she told the room, "Much stronger, and the rhythm is better."

Archambeau stepped into the king's line of eyesight.

"Dr. LaRue is doing her best to help you. Can you speak?"

"Pain," he mumbled.

"Yes, I imagine so," said Charlotte clinically. "I'd give you morphine, but who knows how that would react to what you've taken at this stage? Let's make sure you're improving first. No. Don't get up. Stay where you are."

Over the doctor's shoulder, the duke asked him, "You became sick after eating?"

King Guénard squinted at Archambeau's question, because of the pain or from concentrating. "Yaas..."

"He needs a lot of water. We need to flush this stuff out." Simon scrambled to obey, while Charlotte checked his heart rate again. "Open up and let me see your tongue, Your Majesty."

When she poked it with a needle, he cried, "Ouch!"

Taking his hand in hers, she pressed her nails into his thick fingers. "Do you feel that?"

"Of course. Stop it." His voice was growing stronger.

"Good. The numbness is receding. Take this, rinse, and spit it out. We don't want any trace of that poison left in your mouth."

"Poison!" The king's eyes bulged, alarmed.

"We do not believe your illness was without provocation, Your Majesty," said Archambeau. "The doctor believes there was poison in the food sent up to this room. That may or may not have reacted with your patent medicine."

The king tried again to rise, and Charlotte pressed on his shoulder to keep him down. It clearly took little effort, for he was as weak as a newborn lamb. Charlotte handed the king another glass of water passed to her by Simon. "Drink this down. I want to see you consuming one every half hour. We need this stuff out of your body as soon as possible."

Over her head, Archambeau asked the king a battery of questions. "How many of these after-dinner treats have arrived here? And from whom? How did they know you would want them?"

The king made a helpless gesture with his hands towards his servant. "Tell him."

Simon nervously wrung his hands together. "The first night we arrived, two days before the competition began, we received several dishes, each with a card."

"Who delivered it?"

"I don't know! It was just waiting for us outside the door on a tray!"

Archambeau went back to investigating the table and flipped over a small white card. "Gerhard Perdersen."

"No!" I protested. "He would never!"

He ignored me and went back to his interrogation of Simon. "How did these bribes arrive?"

"They weren't bribes!"

"What do you call them? During the Winter Revels, the king is not to have any contact with the competitors. Who planned this?"

At this delicate point in the interrogation, King Guénard closed his eyes and gave a slight moan. The duke didn't spare him a glance, but kept his predatory gaze upon the hapless aide. "Answer me, Simon, and don't look to His Majesty for answers. I'm in charge of his security, and I'm sure you know how I deal with those reluctant to answer my questions."

"I might have let it slip that His Majesty has a weakness for sweets. But it was an innocent remark that I made in passing."

"To whom?"

"A servant girl. Someone here at the villa? It was a musical name. I asked her if there was a bakery or sweet shop in Vouvant."

"How many times has Chef Perdersen sent something?"

His brow wrinkled. "This was the first one from that chef. The others were Beinhouwer and Faucher."

Archambeau drew me aside. "I would like Dr. LaRue to stay here for the evening. I will send a telegram to his personal physician, but for now, we need to keep what occurred here quiet."

I nodded in agreement. "Let me go to our room, and I'll bring back a few of Dr. LaRue's things."

"Wait." Archambeau's hand on my arm stopped me. "What can you tell me about Chef Perdersen?"

"That he would never poison His Majesty. He isn't a revolutionary. All he cares about is preparing the best food in Alenbonné."

"People are not always what they show on the surface, Elinor."

Angered, I shook off his hold. "If you don't trust my opinion, why ask me?"

"I shall have to question him."

"That is fair, but I want to be there."

"Then hurry and get your friend's things, and dress yourself. That nightgown is far too revealing."

Chapter Ten

By the time I returned to the king's room, the sun was making a pink outline of the hills. I passed a chambermaid, only to realize it was Mys Melody Cantrell. We exchanged a brief hello and smile, for she was off to do her morning's work and I had my own plans.

When I gave the same knock sequence, the duke had done earlier, he opened the king's door to me. King Guénard was in bed with his eyes closed, either asleep or exhausted. Charlotte was giving instructions to the king's man. "He needs to be kept quiet, and he won't be up to anything for days. Forget him attending the Winter Revels."

Archambeau interrupted. "We will come up with an excuse for the king's absence, and Count Westergaard can play host. To end the celebration would cause too many rumors."

Charlotte shrugged. "As long as His Majesty keeps quiet, I'm fine with that. Naturally, I'll stay here until his own doctor can look after him."

"I've sent a coded telegraph to him through a servant. He's coming on an express and should be here within a few hours."

"Good. Now, he needs to drink as much water as we can force

down him. We've got to get the plumbing moving to flush out the poison."

"Thank you for all your efforts, doctor."

"To tell you the truth, heart disease in the living isn't my specialty, though I've seen enough of it on the dissection table." She gave the sleeping king a speculative look. "It would be interesting to see, strictly from a technical point of view—"

I interrupted her before she could put in a request for the king's corpse. "Here are your clothes, Charlotte." To the duke, I added, "Are you going to question Chef Perdersen or not?"

With the immediate crisis past, Archambeau was more at ease, though his shoulders still held tension. "Eager to see your favorite? Then we shall go roust him out of bed. But first I need a change of clothes myself. Come along, Chalamet."

Archambeau's room was just a few doors down the hall from the king. When we entered, the astonished eyes of the duke's valet greeted us.

"Don't mind Madame Chalamet, Luca. She's working with me."

The man's face became blank as he murmured, "Yes, Your Grace."

The duke's room was a suite, and the two men left me in the parlor area that connected to the bedroom. I wandered about, examining the room with its chairs, sofa, and tables. Even though it had the same genteel shabbiness as our own, the furniture was in better shape, and the wallpaper didn't smell of mildew. The window looked down into the side gardens; this side of the wing must be west facing, thus making the king's bedroom the corner suite.

They left the adjoining door open; I saw Archambeau's evening suit tossed on the bed, though the two men were out of view. But as I moved restlessly around the room, I discovered a dressing mirror in the corner which reflected through the doorway at such an angle that I could see the duke standing in his trousers, pulling on a fresh shirt.

Well.

It took a moment for me to turn around and break my appreciative stare.

His voice reached me easily. "Tell me what you know of Perdersen."

"Perdersen's been at the Crown Hotel for over twenty years, where he started as a pastry cook but was quickly promoted because of his talent. He's well-respected, though some staff think he can be a hard taskmaster. Always on time. A hard worker. Dedicated. Not someone who is going to take it into their head to poi— do what you think."

"A shave, Your Grace?" asked Luca, smoothly ignoring my misstep.

"It will have to wait." To me, he said, "What are his politics?"

"None that I know of. He isn't an anarchist, if that's what you are implying."

He emerged from the bedroom dressed in a dark navy-blue suit with a thin, pale gray stripe and a dove-gray satin necktie held fast with a sapphire pin. His cuff links were golden and his shoes had a mirror finish. While his thick, wavy hair was in place, the shadow on his cheeks hinted at some disruption. It made him a bit more human.

Pulling his cuffs down to sort his sleeves under his coat, he said, "You know nothing of the man himself. His hates; his loves. What does the man do during his free time? Who are his friends? Where does he drink? Does he gamble?"

"I may not know the particulars about his favorite color, or if he puts his left sock on before the right, but I do know his measure. He is not a revolutionary."

Archambeau's look was condescending, which irritated me.

"What do you think a traitor to the king looks like? Do you think he has a long, dark mustache that he twirls as he skulks around in a cape, hiding in the shadows? Life isn't a melodrama. No. Dissidents are everyday people, leading ordinary lives, until they betray you."

He started searching through the drawers of the room's desk. Locating a leather pouch, he slipped it into his interior coat pocket.

"We shall begin our investigation with Perdersen's apartments."

As we exited, the duke turned on his heel and walked confidently off towards the main stairwell. Across the hall, a door opened, and I met the dismayed eyes of his sister, Lady Valentina Fontaine.

"Coming, Chalamet?"

I trotted after him, feeling her stare pierce my back.

It turned out that Archambeau had knowledge of where everyone was housed. It was thus simple for him to go down the back servant stairs and take a service corridor into another building, which was the barn converted to be used for the Winter Revels. Here the serving staff and the competition kitchens were located. In less than ten minutes, we were standing in front of a closed door to the sleeping quarters of Chef Perdersen.

When a knock didn't gain a response and a twist on the doorknob showed the room to be locked, Archambeau pulled out the flat pouch he had pocketed earlier. Unrolling the leather displayed a nice set of lock-pick tools. Within a moment, he had the old lock released, and we found the room empty. I gave a sigh of relief.

Archambeau slipped the tools back into their case. "Fled?"

"Today is his day to compete. He's probably already in the kitchen prepping for the day."

"This early in the morning?"

"You clearly don't understand how complicated it is to prepare the dishes you ate last night."

Archambeau showed he was no stranger to searching a room, and did it meticulously and efficiently. He left nothing to chance, and nothing was out of place when he finished.

While he sorted through the wooden wardrobe situated in a corner, I went over to look at the papers tacked to the wall. It was a menu list with ingredients and notes; probably what Perdersen planned on serving tonight. I reached up and took a piece of paper down to inspect it.

"Are you going to stand there or help?"

"I'm reading through the chef's notes for tonight's dinner. Funny, I don't see arsenic on the ingredient list."

"Ha-ha, Chalamet."

"You seem testy. Disappointed not to find any poison, Your Grace?"

He shut the drawer of the dresser rather firmly. "Time to see if your favorite is in the kitchen, as you believe, or if has run for the Zulskayan hills."

As the duke moved behind me to the door, I folded the paper quickly and put it into my pocket. There was no need for Archambeau to see the rude political cartoon I had found of a worker kicking the king's arse as he bent over to grab a crown on the ground. It would only prejudice him against the chef.

As I'd guessed, we found Chef Perdersen in one of three kitchens being used for the competition. He was overseeing the staff, who were prepping vegetables and kneading dough. To my relief, he was no monster, but only the same man I had always known: middle-aged, with a rather fleshy, dough-loaf body and jowls that quivered as he smelled the stock simmering on the stove.

Prowling his domain, he stopped in front of one young woman chopping an onion. "No. No. All should be the same size. Watch." He took the knife from her and chopped the onion rapidly. "See."

Noticing our entrance, he returned the knife to his assistant, handle first, and, wiping his hands, came over to greet us. "Madame Chalamet. I apologize for not speaking with you on the first night."

"No need to apologize. You were being swarmed with admirers! I can't wait to taste what you have for us tonight."

At my words, his smile grew to a grin and his dark raisin eyes danced with excitement. "It will be perfection! Tonight, you will have a masterpiece that will amaze and delight your tongue as nothing has before."

I introduced the men. "Duke de Archambeau, Chef Gerhard Perdersen of the Crown Hotel. I know you are very busy, but we need to speak with you privately if you can spare some time?"

He looked around the kitchen, surveying the work by his two assistants before beckoning us to follow him to a quiet corner. "Yes? How can I help you?"

Archambeau didn't hesitate. "When did you gain access to a kitchen here at Lindengaard?"

The chef suddenly grew more interested in us. "So you are here about my complaint?"

"What complaint?" the duke countered.

"Chef Beinhouwer—"

"That's one of the private chefs who competed last night," I told Archambeau, who gave me a curt nod before urging Perdersen to continue his story.

"Beinhouwer squatted in this kitchen all night! He even refused the unloading of my groceries, so those had to be in the cellar until about an hour ago. So petty. But what can you expect from a man who salts before tasting? Who thinks tricks will win him this competition? He has held a grudge against me ever since the Crown promoted me instead of him as head chef."

"But you had access to prepare food here the first day, did you not?" asked the duke.

"Yes, but so did the others. Beinhouwer and Faucher almost

came to blows that evening over the use of the stove in kitchen two."

"Faucher is the Royal Hotel chef that competes tonight against Chef Perdersen," I explained to the duke.

"Beinhouwer makes enemies easily, for he believes himself god-like," said Gerhard.

"It's come to my attention that there was food sent to the king these last two nights from the chefs."

Perdersen nodded sagely. "Ah, so you are here about the bribes! I told the others they were foolish to be sending things to King Guénard. Perhaps it was a trap? To see who would bend the rules? But if not, His Majesty is not the only one who judges us, so what good does it do to bribe one? It is the people, people like Madame Chalamet, who cast their votes. It was a waste of time and sugar."

"Are you saying you sent nothing to the king?"

"Certainly not! I do not have to cheat, to worm my way into his affections. Tonight my dinner shall be like fireworks, glorious, shining. A greatness that you cannot ignore. What need do I have for such pathetic games? I leave that to the likes of the others who doubt their talent."

Perhaps it was my expression that made Gerhard realize things were far more serious. He paused. "Why do you ask these questions about food? Did someone break out in a rash or puke in a bucket? You cannot lay the blame on me, no matter what Beinhouwer says! I sent nothing."

I was ready to believe him, but the duke was not so trusting.

"Where were you last night from about 11 p.m. to 4 a.m.?"

It would have been best for the chef's innocence if the red flush that spread over his dome head hadn't been so obvious. He was clearly flustered and uneasy by the duke's question.

"When I saw Beinhouwer would not give me use of my kitchen, I left."

"Where did you go?"

"It is none of your business what I do outside the kitchen,

mysir de duke. I may be a common man, but who are you to ask these questions? A guardia? Are we policing the preparation of food now?"

Perdersen was growing angry, which meant he would say something he'd later regret. I tried to soothe him. "Chef, His Grace is the king's man. He is here in his official capacity. I know it might embarrass you to answer these questions, but believe me, it is incredibly important. He is not accusing anyone of anything, but just trying to discover where you were."

Gerhard's eyes swiveled around the room, looking for an escape, but there was none. Archambeau's tall form was imposing, and he would not let his fish wriggle off the hook. Sighing, Gerhard drew closer and said in a much lower voice, "Fine. Fine. I was with mysir Faucher the entire evening. Ask him."

"In his room? Only I noticed that your bed hadn't been slept in, and your cheeks were not shaved this morning."

"Yes. *Yes*. All night. In his room. I don't know why you need to know about my love life—"

"I knew it! Liar! Philanderer!" A scream made everyone freeze as the ghostly shade of Claude Frossard formed behind Gerhard.

The Noise Ghost swept through the kitchen like a storm. Knives danced out of their sorting blocks; pans shimmied on tables. Shocked and terrified, the staff dived for the back door, running as if their lives depended on their escape.

"Oh, no!" I cried. "I thought we left Claude at the Crown! How did he get here?"

"I followed him!" screeched Gerhard's dead lover. "I knew I couldn't trust him. That he was lying. You can't fool me!"

"Not another one!" Archambeau grabbed my arm and dragged me towards the door.

"No, I have to help Gerhard," I protested, trying to get my wrist free from his iron grip.

"I'm not getting possessed again. Once was more than enough!"

"You never really loved me!" shouted Claude.

Gerhard finally woke up from his stupor. He yelled back. "You cling like a barnacle! Leave me alone to live my life!"

"Your life? You want your life back? So do I!"

A flat-bottomed saucepan, along with its contents, came flying across the room, spraying tomato sauce on the walls before hitting Gerhard smack in the middle of his forehead. The chef collapsed to the floor, and the kitchen became quiet.

When he didn't rise, Claude came to hover over him, wringing his hands. "Gerhard, I didn't mean it. Speak to me!"

I was about to rush to Perdersen's aid when he groaned.

"See, your favorite isn't dead." And with that, Archambeau dragged me away.

Chapter Eleven

In the corridor, we both started to argue.

"See, I told you he had nothing to do with this!"

"That remains to be seen. Someone knew about these bedtime treats and used them to their advantage. Chef Perdersen could have made the dessert before he came here and brought it with him."

"Anyone could have done that! We know Simon spoke to a maid. Who else knew the chefs were dropping off food at the king's door? It sounds like it was an open secret among the chefs."

Bringing me into a stairwell, Archambeau looked all directions before replying. "I agree. And don't think I have let Simon off the hook. He is being replaced with a man I can trust and being sent back to Alenbonné on the first train. Now, Chalamet, I need you—"

"Yes!" I interrupted eagerly.

"—to keep quiet."

Crossing my arms, I said, "Is that all you think I can do? After what I did at the Nightingale?"

"This has nothing to do with ghosts or stolen tiaras, but is a cold-blooded attempted murder upon our rightful sovereign. This is my field, not yours. Now, first, I need to talk with Count Westergaard."

"You need a cover story, a plausible lie about why King Guénard won't be attending."

"Exactly. It will be a migraine. He uses that excuse whenever he doesn't want to attend a function. Everyone will accept it easily enough."

"But no visitors except his doctor, to keep the would-be poisoner in the dark about whether his—"

"Or her—"

"—plan worked and how well."

"He will need a food taster."

"I shall send a runner out anonymously for food. A runner who will taste it before he hands it over."

"But you can't send too much food, or the poisoner might think the king is well and try again."

He tapped my nose with his forefinger. "The way you go on, someone might think you are an expert liar."

"Duplicity is not unknown to Ghost Talkers. Sometimes our patrons even want it."

"You need to leave it to me for now." When I didn't answer, he said warningly, "Chalamet..."

"Since you don't need me, I have things to do today. Such as an assignation in the garden with a man."

Before he could ask who, I left.

A Lindengaard footman stopped me. He had the parcel from the bank that I had requested yesterday. Back upstairs, I found our room empty. It was still too early to meet Marson, so lying down on my bed, I laced my fingers over my stomach and stared at the ceiling to think. A few hours later, Charlotte entered.

"I'm as beaten as a rug," she said through a yawn as she collapsed onto her own bed. "His physician is here now, and I've handed the royal pain in the arse over to him. Good riddance! If you can believe it, he was already whining about not being able to eat when I was leaving!"

"Oh, Charlotte, is he going to recover?"

"Too soon to tell. Could be liver damage; however, that's now the royal physician's problem. He showed me the door quickly enough. But there's another complication."

"What?"

"I tested the Dr. Lilly's powder, and it's almost pure potassium chloride."

"Not good, I suspect?"

"No. In that form, it's another poison. I passed that information along to His Grace. He didn't look pleased to know." She punched her pillow and, finding her sleeping mask on the table beside her bed, pulled it over her forehead. "I'm going back to sleep. If anyone wants me, tell them I've gone back to Alenbonné."

"Oh, Charlotte," I murmured again with a smile, but she didn't answer. Her breathing had already deepened with sleep. In a moment, while thinking over all the things I needed to do, I did the same.

It wasn't until light shafted in through the window at a certain angle that I woke up. Rolling over, I picked up my father's watch, resting on the bedside table. I had had it repaired, smoothing out the dents and replacing the gems. Seeing that it was well past lunch, I leapt out of bed. If I wanted to meet the Marson family in the formal gardens, I needed to hurry.

My outfit was sadly rumpled, but I didn't have time to change. Cold water at the washstand served as a restorative. In the mirror, I hastily redid my hair, setting a fresh bun. There is nothing like jewelry to make a woman feel herself, so I quickly selected pear-shaped pearl drop earrings and a ruby pin for my neck scarf.

My father's watch I put into my left pocket, and, after loading my small pistol, tucked it into my right. After the attempt on the king's life, I planned to keep my man-stopper with me.

The terraced gardens of Lindengaard were marked out in squares, triangles, and diamonds. The count must have spent his money here and not on the house's interior, for there was plenty to admire: evergreen topiaries shaped like mythical animals, a centerpiece fountain, and a lily pond with plenty of plump ornamental fish.

I found the widow and her son sitting in an arbor, the thick vines shading it even though the grapes were long gone. Madame Marson was knitting, sitting sideways on a bench so her back was to her son; he was leaning against a post, looking out over the gently rolling hills marked with vineyard rows.

"What a beautiful view," I said, entering the shelter with its dappled shade.

"It is," said Mysir Marson. He cast a sideways glance at his mother. However, she remained silent, eyes cast down on the work in her hands.

"After the gray skies of Alenbonné, I find the Vouvant climate to be invigorating," I commented.

"Stop it!" snapped Madame Marson. Rising, her knitting forgotten, she pointed her needles at me and said, "I know the real reason you're here!"

In my line of work, I have met many people who were angry, hysterical, and sometimes even violent. When facing such a storm, the first thing to remember is to remain calm. I came no closer to her, but neither did I give ground. Showing weakness was not a good idea, either.

The next thing to do was to get them talking. Keeping my voice neutral, I asked, "Why do you think I'm here, Madame Marson?"

"Don't think I haven't heard about you, Madame Chalamet. How you bespelled that poor girl in a cake shop yesterday!"

"Do you mean Mys Cynthia Benard? Yes, I did her a small favor yesterday."

"You admit it?!"

"Why not? The girl met her dead brother and healed old wounds. I'm sure we can find her in town, if you wish to speak directly to her about what occurred between us. Or we can speak to her cousin, Mys Melody Cantrell, who works here at Lindengaard as a house servant. It's always best to seek facts from those who are involved rather than listen to rumors that too often exaggerate."

Like an agitated bull pestered by flies, Madame Marson didn't know who to charge to relieve her torment. My calm manner seemed to baffle her, so she turned her anger toward her son. "He wants me admitted. To a sanatorium."

"I have never suggested that!" declared Marson. "Only that we discuss your health with a doctor. Nothing more."

"Your son has not asked me to do anything of that nature," I said reassuringly.

She retreated to her seat, clutching the knitting needles in her hands like weapons. "If you're so clever, you do the talking."

"I would like to hear more about your husband."

"So you can play your party games, Ghost Talker?" she sneered. "Let me tell you, I didn't listen to Parnell Lafayette and I won't listen to you."

I ignored the ghost of Harry Marson standing next to his wife, his face and hands begging her to listen to me. If Madame Marson was ghost-blind, I would have to resort to other tactics to get her to come around.

"Your son told me you almost died when he was born."

Her face softened momentarily before hardening again. "That's true. I almost died, and if it hadn't been for my Harry looking after me day and night, I wouldn't have survived. It's all due to him I'm here today."

"He must have cared for you deeply."

"He always looked after me. Doctors, medicine, specialists, trips to the south during the winter, all to help me get stronger."

"It must have worked. You look healthy as a horse."

Behind me, her son hid his smile behind his hand.

"If I'm healthy today, it's because Harry's love pulled me through."

I looked down at my nails, hiding the intensity of my gaze with my eyelashes. When Marson had told me that his mother had grown hysterical when Parnell told her information about her husband, it had made me wonder about the true state of their marriage— especially as guilt seemed to play such an integral part. It was time to strike and see if my guess was correct.

"You speak much of your husband's love and care for you, but what did you return to him?"

"I don't know what you mean!?" She stamped her foot at my words. Her eyes should have been weeping at my accusation, not blazing defiance.

Aha! Yes, I think I have your mettle now, Madame Marson! I twirled my finger in the air. "His death. Were you relieved when they brought you the news? These widow weeds? A show. Theater. Dressing for the public to believe in the performance. You feel guilty about it, don't you? Guilty for not caring?"

Under her powder, her complexion turned as white as bleached bone, the rouge on her cheeks standing out harshly like a porcelain doll's face. Madame Marson's voice cracked. "Leave me! You don't know what you are talking about. Herkel, send her away!"

I gave a parting shot. "I'd be careful, Madame Marson. Your husband is here, and he will have his revenge."

∽

I found Mys Melody Cantrell cleaning guest rooms. She was eager to talk but didn't stop her work, moving around the room with her feather duster. The girl was obviously not in charge of our rooms.

"Oh, madame! Cynthia is like a different person. I mean, she's always been sweet and nice, but now—" The young girl scrunched her nose, thinking. "Now, it's like she's awakened from a dream. I don't know how to explain the change, but we've all noticed it. It's like she's a bright, shiny penny."

"I'm glad to hear that."

"Her parents would love to thank you if you have the time. They are downstairs setting up the tables for tonight. Would you like me to take you to them?"

"That would be most helpful."

She finished her work, and we started down the servant stairs together.

I asked, "Do you think you could do a personal favor for me?"

"Anything, madame."

"My hair. I really need help with it tonight."

She giggled. "Oh, I can do that! I'm done with my day here in about three more hours, if that suits?"

Downstairs, she brought me to the dining hall to introduce me to Madame and Mysir Benard, salt-of-the-earth, hard-working folk, native to Vouvant. Both shook my hand so hard that my head bobbed up and down.

"Our poor girl," said Mysir Benard.

"Always sad under her happiness," said Madame Benard.

"But no more," said the girl's father.

"No indeed, and that is all thanks to the magic you worked upon her," said Cynthia's mother. "We've told everyone we've met that Madame Chalamet is the real deal. No false coin."

Thinking of what Madame Marson said in the garden, I replied with a smile, "So I've heard. Now, I was wondering—"

When I paused, they both asked eagerly, "Yes?"

"Just like your daughter, there is someone at Lindengaard who needs my help. You could help her find peace also, if you don't mind helping me."

"What can we do?" the three asked me eagerly.

Chapter Twelve

That evening, when we entered the dining room, Charlotte and I separated to different tables again. Truthfully, it irritated me, so I was lost in my thoughts when a hand brushed the back of my chair and Mysir de Archambeau took the seat next to mine.

"Shouldn't you be up there at the king's table?" I demanded.

"There is no king's table tonight, because he's come down with a migraine and is under the care of his personal physician," he said blandly. "Do I recognize that dress?"

"It's a style called the Nightingale."

Across the table, his sister sat down, saying crossly, "What are you two smiling about?"

Lady Valentina Fontaine wore a gown of burnt-orange satin, the cloth layered across the chest in an X, adding padding to a nonexistent bosom. Her choice of jewelry was diamonds in the ears and a matching necklace.

Well, I still preferred my gray-mist pearls with the diamond spacers. It had been a gift from my father, and one of the few pieces that had escaped being stolen the night of his murder. They always comforted me when I touched them, as I did now.

The room was filling up with guests, and from the corner of my eye I saw a black velvet dress go by, escorted by Herkel Marson. I was uncertain how he had convinced his mother to come, but I imagined that my forged note written on the king's stationary, which Charlotte had purloined for me earlier in the day, had helped.

As a suppressed shriek made all heads turn towards the Marsons, I hid my smile behind my napkin. Herkel had picked up a book resting on his mother's chair and now seemed to be in an intense discussion with his mother.

I picked up my menu card and read it, shielding my face from the duke's sister while I asked him, "Did your investigation turn up anything?"

"Mostly no. But I will not discuss it here and now."

"Why not?"

"Because for the next few hours, I wish to enjoy my food and not think about what could be in it that could kill me."

"Oh."

At the head table, Count Westergaard stood up and started making a speech, explaining the king's absence. He wasn't an especially talented speaker and went on for too long, expressing rather incoherently that he was happy to host, while still sorry for the king's illness. There was a long drone about the importance of the monarchy, and how King Guénard's leadership protected Sarnesse from her enemies, while cementing bonds of friendship with those who deserved it. So it was no surprise that his guests were growing restless as the count's stumbling oration delayed the first course.

Finally, someone was brave enough to give a little tug on his tailcoat. With a rushed ending to his speech, Count Westergaard finally sat down and signaled the wait staff to begin serving.

If I was hoping to see a guilty face in response to the news that the king would not be joining us, I was disappointed. The diners were more interested in the wine the servers were bringing out to toast the king's health than his actual well being.

To the duke I said, "I noticed last night that all the bottles were the Lindengaard label. No Chambaux?"

"No. The king deliberately had the Winter Revels here so that Count Westergaard could make some sales once people tasted his stock. Many who received tickets are wine connoisseurs, so I expect a lot of bottles will go home in crates when the Revels finish."

Lady Valentina, who had been straining to hear our conversation, interjected. "While the count's vineyards are passable, they do not produce quality on the level of what Chambaux produces."

The duke said diplomatically, "With proper management and time, Lindengaard might surprise you."

"What do you mean?"

"It needs a financial investment to improve things, an investment of capital the count lacks."

The traditional first course of soup arrived. I knew immediately that the beef consommé garnished with carrots and turnips, with its moist but plump dumplings sprinkled with fresh chopped chervil, was Chef Perdersen's. I was familiar with it from the Crown.

"Are you going to judge fairly, Chalamet? Or have you already picked sides?"

"Of course I shall be fair with my comments! Besides, this turtle soup is not the best version I've ever tasted. It needs more seasoning, or perhaps the poor turtle wasn't fresh."

Luckily for us, Lady Valentina's partner distracted her partner by claiming an acquaintance.

Archambeau speculated. "Maybe romance has thrown Chef Faucher off his game?"

"By that logic, it should be Chef Perdersen who suffers. After all, he was the one who got his head dented with a pot today."

"I think the man must thrive under adversity, or so says the woman I've put in his kitchen."

"You have a spy on his team?"

"No, a guard while Simon is serving as food taster. I've got another man watching Chef Faucher. We don't need any food tainted or accusations that there are favorites flying about. I have reprimanded everyone and reminded them that any more of this nonsense of sending treats to King Guénard shall disqualify them all."

The second course was red snapper and baked mackerel. The grilled red snapper came with a herb butter and roasted slices of lemon. It had a delicious nutty flavor and melted in my mouth. The mackerel was a dark-fleshed fish with rather an oily taste. The chef had smothered it with a creamy aioli, mushrooms, and cheese.

"Faucher really is doing poorly tonight," I commented quietly to my companion.

"How do you know the mackerel is Faucher's?"

"How do you know I meant the mackerel?" I countered. "If you know your chef as well as I do, their food is as definitive as a fingerprint. That's why I knew the dessert was not from Chef Perdersen. The entire thing was clearly an amateur effort far below what he would do on his worst day."

"That's what Perdersen said." At my expression, he said, "Surprised, Chalamet? When things calmed down, I went back later and discussed it with him. He lectured me about why it was poor quality and how it would have been beneath him to serve it. Something about the bottom of the pastry being wet and the presentation being pedestrian. No imagination, is what he said."

I felt smug. Perhaps I would have rubbed my victory in his face but, using a glass of wine to conceal his mouth from the other diners, he added, "I also found a bag of rat poison in the kitchen pantry, right behind the bag labeled 'sugar'."

My fork slid out of my hand onto the plate, making a ting. Thankfully, the noise from the other diners covered my slip.

"So he had means and opportunity, but why would he do it? And it proves that the other chefs would also have access."

"Quick to defend him, aren't you?"

The next course was a chicken pie with buttery crust

competing against glazed ham. Trying to keep my focus on the food, I said to Archambeau, "Notice how Chef Perdersen has built his courses? None of them heavy? All of them following a culinary theme?"

"The way to win your heart, madame, is to hire the best cook in the land. You would abandon those high principles of yours for a pastry cream puff, a juicy roasted haunch, or a buttered potato."

I paused, seriously weighing the idea of marrying someone just to have Chef Perdersen as my personal chef. "I admit it would be tempting, but Gerhard would never leave the Crown. He's adored there, and his ego needs the adulation of the public, not just one person."

"So, who is this man you met in the garden?"

"No one you know."

"Is it possibly the well-mustached gentleman known as Mysir Marson?" His gaze swiveled across the room to where mother and son were sitting just a table away.

"Do you have a spy watching me, also?"

"No, *I'm* watching you, and you've been surreptitiously eyeing the Marson family ever since they entered the dining hall. I noticed you were with them for some time the first night. It makes me wonder why they have your interest."

"Madame Marson is a widow."

"That I gained from her overdone black. If she is in the throes of such a paralyzing grief, I marvel that she's been able to bless us with her presence at dinner."

I blushed. "Perhaps the king sent her an encouraging note?"

"Indeed? And what did this correspondence say?"

Luckily, I didn't have to answer; our friendliness had rankled his sister. "Whatever are you two whispering about?"

Before we could answer, Lady Valentina started a barrage of questions at her brother about people she and Archambeau knew in society. Had he spoken yet with Victor Bankston, who was attending? The youngest son of the Lord of Monteville? And wasn't Lady Cleevedon wearing the most enchanting gown tonight? If they were lucky, perhaps she would play the piano tonight after dinner?

Each inquiry began with a "Madame Chalamet probably wouldn't know Lord so-and-so," or "Remember when we had the Zulskayan ambassador over?" Unfortunately, it didn't have quite the effect she had hoped for, as the duke would stop and explain who they were to me every time she brought up a new name. By the time the course finished, her fork had savaged her duck, making it look like a wild animal had attacked it in a killing frenzy.

Because I was waiting for it, my sharp ears caught a ping: the sound of a coin touching a plate. The show was about to begin.

In a moment, there were dozens of clink-ping-clinks as coins fell from the air. They struck glasses, dinnerware, or bounced onto the parquet floor. Confused guests looked about for an explanation. A few sprang from their seats, gazing up to the ceiling to see where the coins were coming from, while others simply exclaimed in excitement as they picked them up from where they had fallen.

Lady Valentina, who had turned at the commotion, observed, "Whatever is happening at that table?"

"Ah, the Marson's table. What a coincidence," said Archambeau sarcastically.

The man seated beside Lady Valentina said, "It must be something to amuse the guests, though I never figured Westergaard for a clever man. Dull as ditchwater, in fact. Learned, you know. Not one to bother himself about planning an entertaining party. He only got the Winter Revels here because he's the king's cousin."

Count Westergaard looked nothing but perplexed. He stopped a server and was having a conversation about the issue when the mysterious rain of coins ceased.

Conversation around the room re-started when someone exclaimed loudly, "All of them have the same date!"

"How strange," I heard one lady say as she leaned over to her partner, who was holding another coin.

"The same as yours," he replied, holding it up for her to see.

As more and more discussed the strangeness of the thirty-year-old coins, Madame Marson grew more agitated. Her shrill voice reached my ears as she spoke rapidly to her son, who was trying ineffectively to calm her. "First the book! The book that I sent Harry to get. Now these coins from the year we married!"

She stood up and slapped her son's hands away before storming out of the room. He gave a hasty apology to his tablemates, before following her.

The duke leaned over to me. "This has the hallmark of your work, Chalamet."

"What do you mean?" asked his sister from across the table.

"If there is drama, be sure our resident Ghost Talker is involved."

"I can't wait for dessert. I wonder what it will be?" was my innocent reply.

Chapter Thirteen

The next day, Charlotte planned to attend a day trip arranged for the Winter Revel guests to some nearby castle ruins.

"But why take your medical bag?"

"I assure you that before the day is out, plenty of society ladies will need the services of a doctor, Elinor."

"How can you know that?" I asked as she looked in a mirror, tying her stock around her throat.

"Oh, there'll be the ladies who won't wear a stout boot, so will twist their ankle in a hole wearing a slipper. Especially if some man they favor is hanging about nearby. That doesn't include the ones who don't take regular exercise and exhaust themselves with climbing. There are bound to be spiders and snakes. Someone will get bitten, I guarantee it."

"You seem positively gleeful about all these supposed catastrophes!"

"I don't make misfortunes happen. Stupid people do that. But I would call myself foolish not to take advantage of idiots." She pulled on her coat. "Why don't you come with me? Get away from here for a bit? Bound to be some spirits hanging about the old ruins. I'm told they withstood some invasion ending with every local man slaughtered."

"I think staying here and reading a book sounds far more comfortable than risking snakes, spiders, and turned ankles."

"Well then, enjoy."

After the carriages left for the ruins, I made my way downstairs to the library, where the day before, I had filched the book which the servants had placed on Madame Marson's dinner chair. It was pure luck that I had found it. I wondered what she would think when it turned back up on her pillow tonight.

When I entered the Lindengaard library, the lord of the manor, Count Westergaard, was standing near the window. He was discussing something about the vineyard with a man whom I assumed, by his dress, to be his estate manager.

I turned to leave them in peace, but Count Westergaard spoke out, asking me to stay. "I'm afraid I didn't have time to greet you properly when you arrived, Madame Chalamet."

"The Duchesse de Chambaux and her daughter needed your attention more than I."

At the mention of the duchesse's title, he stiffened. A small man with narrow shoulders, his discomfort was obvious as his hand reached up to readjust his thin wire spectacles. He forced himself to smile and remarked, "Some of these new families think they can run over the rest of us."

"Oh, I don't know that I would call the Chambaux line new," I protested.

"My dear madame, Sarnesse royal genealogy is my life's work. The Chambaux duchy is less than two hundred years old. My own well-documented ancestral lineage is triple their age." His rounded shoulders straightened with pride, and his chin raised. "Let me have the pleasure of showing you around."

"If you're busy— I don't want to interrupt you—"

He gave a regal glance to his foreman, who gave a quick bow of his head before leaving. The count didn't acknowledge his departure, saying to me, "The library at Lindengaard is my favorite room. The view is quite spectacular, while also being secluded from the rest of the house. It is my retreat from the world, where I am free to indulge my hobbies."

"Do you find us guests tiring, Count?"

"Oh no, I didn't mean that— well, perhaps I did a little." He gave a self-conscious cough, before confiding, "The Winter Revels has tested my powers of being host. Finding something interesting for everyone to do every day is more challenging than I imagined."

Looking around the book-lined walls, I saw an ancient marble hearth (large enough that I could have walked inside), thick old rugs, and heavy oak furniture with very stiff backs. It was a weighty room, one steeped in the pompous formality of long ago years. Perhaps I would have appreciated it more if the drapes were not so threadbare and the rugs didn't have worn spots that furniture lacked to conceal.

Ignoring the signs of noble poverty, I said diplomatically, "You have a very extensive library. Not only the classics, but even the popular works."

"We may be far from the capital, but I like to stay informed," he replied proudly. "It is here that I apply myself to my studies, my life's work."

"I thought the vineyards—?"

"My real passion, Madame Chalamet, is not the dreary farm work that pays the bills, as the vulgar Alenbonné merchants say. It is my research of the royal line, the ancestors from which we can trace all of Sarnesse nobility."

He brought my attention to the glass display cabinets that took center stage in the room. Bending over, he pointed at names inscribed on parchment, and a few other mementos with cards outlining their illustrious anecdotes: medals with faded ribbons and who had won them and where, pocket watches of ancestors, and signet rings carved with royal insignia. He also had an extensive coin collection, where his goal was to have one of every ruler Sarnesse displayed.

"My family has close ties to the Guénard lineage. My great-great-grandmother was the current king's father's older sister. If Sarnesse practiced absolute primogeniture, like Zulskaya, the firstborn, regardless of gender, would have ruled. Instead, we use the agnatic, where a first son takes the crown."

"Imagine, your family could be sitting on the throne."

He gave a little twitter, like a throaty songbird.

"Unlike others, I do not think the responsibility for the kingdom is a simple thing to manage. Certainly King Guénard is finding it a hard row nowadays, with food shortages and unpopular taxation. Besides, fate could have killed my great-grandmother before she married, or had my father marry someone else than my mother. We are all a victim of these little twists which dictate our life."

At his words about fate and lost opportunities, I immediately thought of my father's murder. Perhaps he sensed my change to a somber mood, for Count Westergaard changed the subject to one lighter in tone. "Meanwhile, I enjoy this wonderful villa and estate with its colorful history. It has seen many dramas, both royal and pedestrian, over the centuries. Plenty of ghosts for someone in your field to explore. It is indeed a privilege to look after the ancient heritage of Lindengaard. Come, let me show you."

Seeing he had a captive audience, he spent an hour bringing out the house plans, which documented the subsequent additions or remodels. Hearing the estate's history, it made me wonder how many ghosts I'd find if I did a survey. It also made me itch to get a bucket of paint, new wallpaper, and fabrics to bring every room up to date. I did not mention my desire to redecorate, thinking it wouldn't be taken in good spirit, and kept my remarks to admiring ones.

"What does this line mean?" I pointed to an area on the Lindengaard floor plan that confused me.

He twittered again and put a finger over his lips. "It's a secret passage."

"Oh, is that common with old houses? I saw a secret passage at the Duke de Archambeau's house in Alenbonné."

He bristled. "Not the same thing, and surely not as grand. Let me show you."

He went and closed the library door, locking it. Returning to an area to the left of the fireplace, his hand went to the side of some of the carved moulding and released a catch. A small, narrow gap appeared.

"Oh, my!" I came to his side and peered in.

"Do you want to explore?"

"Naturally. How could I resist?"

He took an oil lamp down from the mantle and lit it. "It's a tight squeeze, but widens after you get past the fireplace." Probably because we were both short, I didn't find the confines of the passage too bad, though I had to move sideways into a corner.

"Where does it go?"

He replied over his shoulder, "This passage goes down the length of the outside wall and then behind two of the public rooms. One of my ancestors used it to watch and listen in on his guests."

He turned down the flame on his lantern, and I followed, nearly blind. When the count stopped, I stumbled into him.

"Here."

Light made a narrow beam into the darkness of the corridor from the peephole as I heard two familiar voices: Archambeau and his sister, Valentina. They must have stayed behind and not visited the castle ruins.

In my ear, an imp whispered, "Look through this peephole."

Perhaps I should have told my host it was time to turn back, but I couldn't help myself. My horrible curiosity made me bend my eye at it.

Count Westergaard stepped aside so I could gain access. The count must have placed the furniture in a manner to give the peephole-user the best view, for I could clearly see both of the Chambaux siblings. Archambeau looked very dashing in dark blue with black velvet lapels and vest. Lady Valentina wore a deep purple dress with black lace at the cuffs and around the gown's high neck. They were the only two in the room.

"Did it ever occur to you, Val, that sticking your nose into my affairs has never worked out well for you?" The duke's voice sounded irritated and impatient. Though, in my limited experience, it often did when conversing with his sister. She really got under his skin. Perhaps if I'd had siblings, I would have understood their dynamics better, but my younger brother had died along with my mother from the city cough when I was six years old.

Lady Valentina's voice bordered on shrill. "I saw how you looked at her at dinner."

"You always think that any woman I speak to is running after my title. I know you and Josephine have nothing better to do than spit and hiss like old cats, but you really need to get over this need to gossip about matters that don't concern you."

"Don't concern me? Whoever you chose as a partner will affect us all. I have not forgotten what your marriage to Minette did to us, and neither have you. Where is my old brother, the one before Minette got her claws into him? You are distant and cold to us."

"You seem to forget that I married Minette because Mother wanted it. Perhaps that might explain many things about how I treat you both."

The peephole gave a limited view, but I saw Lady Valentina become agitated at his words. "That was Mother, not I. And you could have said no. Men have that power."

"Do I? Because from my vantage point, it did not seem so. Besides, I have no plans to marry again. Once was enough."

The count whispered in my ear, "How interesting, don't you think?"

Rather than being calmed, Lady Valentina's voice grew more strident. "What do you mean to do with her, then? Buying her clothes, inviting her to our house. Now she has followed you here? You have shown her a marked attention, brother."

It was past time to leave, but Count Westergaard's grip on my arm was preventing me from backing up and beating a retreat.

"I think we should leave, for decency's sake," I whispered to him. He didn't seem to hear my plea. In the darkness, his face was as smooth as a cobblestone.

"As you and Mother requested, I had not seen Madame Chalamet for months until that day in the park. And her attendance at the Winter Revels is by the request of King Guénard. Will you next be assigning the king some nefarious purpose for inviting her? As usual, you jump to conclusions."

Lady Valentina sounded close to tears. "I am not exaggerating what I saw with my own eyes! Yesterday morning I saw her leave your room in the early hours of the morning. A tryst right here, under all our noses! What would Mother think? What would your friends say? Even as a mistress you are stooping low, Tristan."

In the darkness, I flushed hotly. Could this grow any more embarrassing? Perhaps le beau idéal set want to discuss their loves publicly, but I did not. If they wanted to have a private conversation shredding my reputation, that was fine, but this conversation was being held before an audience, even though it was a secret. Even an elbow in the count's ribs still didn't get him to move.

"There is a perfectly innocent explanation."

"And that is?" When Archambeau didn't answer her, she spun about so I couldn't see her face, only her heaving shoulders. In a suppressed voice, heavy with emotion, she said, "It's too late, isn't it? She has caught you in her net."

"Again, Val, these matters touch upon the work I do for the crown. I do not discuss King Guénard's business with—" Archambeau's face was unreadable. His expression had returned to that frozen, cold look I disliked so much.

"With family members? I've heard all of that before, Tristan. A very convenient excuse you trot out any time you want to shut down a discussion. Is she your mistress or not?"

"She is not."

"Good. Now promise me you will cut this connection with a jeweler's daughter."

"My business is none of your concern."

"I doubt Mother will feel the same."

A touch of irritation crossed his immobile face. "I know you enjoy the position of concerned sister, Valentina, but you are testing my patience. If I were as stubborn and unreasonable as you and Mother think I am, I would take the woman as my wife just to spite you. Relieve your mind that I have no such notions. I enjoy her company but, as I've said before, we are colleagues who sometimes share common goals. You need to cool your overheated brain."

"I shall tell Mother—"

"Do as you wish. It doesn't change facts."

For a full moment, the two stared at each other, will against will, but it was Lady Valentina who eventually beat a retreat by flouncing from the room. Finally, my host let me go, and I scrambled backwards to leave the passage. My emotions were swinging from embarrassment to outrage.

The lenses of his glasses made his eyes appear reptilian as Count Westergaard said, "That was enlightening. I didn't know you were Mysir Chalamet's daughter. I have some jewels from my ancestors that you might enjoy seeing."

The last thing I wanted to do was look at vintage jewelry. Surely pleading a migraine would be the socially acceptable thing to do, so I could enjoy my humiliation in private.

Chapter Fourteen

Count Westergaard continued chatting about family heirlooms, trying to draw an answer from me. I pleaded a headache to escape.

He was sympathetic. "A dark room, plenty of quiet, and a cool cloth over the eyes is the best medicine."

Bidding him goodbye, I went blindly to the stairs, ready to ascend to freedom, but a hoarse whisper from Mysir Marson stopped me. From a doorway he beckoned me to enter the music room. I hoped it didn't have a secret peephole.

"Mother is hysterical! You must help me!"

His thin, pale face showed a restless night, as did his mustache, which lacked the impeccable grooming of our former meetings. It hung limply, giving his face a defeated, sad appearance.

"Calm yourself, Mysir Marson, and tell me what has happened."

"Last night completely undid her. The book. The coins. Was that you? Did you cause that? Or was it my father, as Mother believes?"

Instead of answering him directly, I prompted, "Take me

through what has been going on since I last met Madame Marson."

He gulped, his fingers twitching in distress.

"After we left you, she was pretty much the same. Disdainful of your kind, and giving me a long lecture about how mediums are charlatans and not to be trusted. She received a note from the king asking her to enjoy the evening's dinner in his place, as he could not attend himself. I was happy to escort her."

So far, all had gone according to my plan. "Go on."

"But when we reached her seat, we found a book on her chair. It gave her a horrible fright, for it was the volume my father was to have picked up for her on the day of his accident. *The Flight of the Songbird*. It was all the rage that year."

"Yes, I remember you telling me that at dinner on our first night here."

"She finally calmed down when dinner started, but by the end of it—" His hazel eyes widened, remembering. "Those coins started falling from the air. Bizarre. Inexplicable. It made little sense at first, until someone pointed out that they had all the same date— the year my parents married."

"Oh my," I clucked sympathetically. Thank goodness the bank had been willing to help me with my odd request about the coins. Probably dropping the Chambaux name was why I got them so quickly.

"My mother became hysterical. When we reached our rooms, she was severely overwrought. Dare I say even feverish? I was so worried, I almost sent for a doctor."

"What exactly did she say? That is incredibly important, Mysir Marson."

"She raved that my father's ghost had returned to wreak his vengeance upon her! Totally outlandish allegations that made no sense. She slept last night with all the gas and candles lit because she fears to see my father's ghost. I think I must end this holiday and take her to see an alienist."

"If you would heed my advice once more, I would keep her here, but ignore her as best as you can. Go about your daily life."

"Following your advice, she has become worse, not better!" Marson drew his fingers through his hair as if ready to pull it out.

"Have you never seen a fever worsen before it breaks, and the patient improves? She is close, very close to healing, and this is part of the process."

He gave me a disbelieving stare.

"People of your mother's type, who hold on to their grief long past a reasonable time, fuel it from feelings other than loss. Your mother's motivations are complicated."

"I don't understand. She really misses my father. He was her everything!"

"I'm sure she misses him, but as years pass, people pick up their life and move onward. She has not. The question is why."

"Why?" he echoed, staring at me.

"I believe your mother's issue springs from a feeling of guilt, for it was she who sent your father on his errand. Her own shame has concocted an idea that he wants vengeance. Has she ever expressed to you the idea that if he had not gone out that day, her husband would still be alive?"

Marson paused for a moment, remembering. "Now that you mention it, she said something like that last night. And a few times right after he died, but I assured her it wasn't her fault. It was an accident that could have happened to anyone, at any time. The drivers in Alenbonné are terrible for taking risks."

"Sometimes, after suffering a great loss, we become fixated. Madame Marson needs to be unstuck."

"But why would evidence that my father has communicated with her from Beyond now make her upset? I thought that was what she wanted! It's why I sent for Mysir Lafayette. I thought she'd be pleased!"

"Your mother has punished herself for years by denying herself the ability to live— to regain happiness— in order to assuage her feeling of guilt. Now that the man she believes she has wronged has returned, she is frightened. Guilt is no longer an abstract notion, but something under the bed and in the dark."

"Not to sound cruel or unfeeling, Madame Chalamet, but he's dead. What could he do?"

I couldn't help but smile as I shook my head. "Mysir Marson, what do you think ghost stories are about? They are nothing but tales of how spirits take their revenge and frighten people near to death."

"But how can—? What will result from all this? I wish now I had never gotten a Ghost Talker involved in our lives."

His bitterness was understandable. In my experience, it wasn't uncommon for those seeking ghosts of their loved ones to find only more pain.

"I would suggest that you go about your normal business. Ignore her hysterics. Let her calm down a bit, and when she asks, as I think she will, to see me, I will be available. Night or day, you may call upon my assistance."

"You would be the last person she will want to see!"

"In times of desperation, you often turn to those you think are your worst enemy. Tell her I am the only person who can release her from Harry's haunting."

After Marson left, I decided to forgo my room and to spend my time investigating.

The floor-plan of the Lindengaard villa was a U-shape. The bottom of the U was the front of the house, and the two branches made separate wings. In the back was a row of barns that were the converted servant quarters and kitchens the chefs were using. These buildings closed the top of the U shape, making a sheltered courtyard area in the center with the tail ends connected to the house.

This formal kitchen garden— a *jardín potager*— had useful plants for food or medicine growing in beds marked out in a pattern of Xs. Despite it being winter, the milder climate in Vouvant, and the shelter from the worst of the weather, allowed lemon and lime trees to continue production. The rosemary and lavender bushes were still green, and I crushed a twig between my fingers to smell their powerful fragrance as I walked down the path.

One kitchen was readying for today's lunch, while the others were under the charge of the restaurant chefs competing tonight: Cadieux and Englehart. The first night had been chefs in private service, and the second the two hotel chefs. The winner of each night would be in the final runoff on the last night.

I wondered how much the construction of these extra kitchens had cost Count Westergaard. Or had the king subsidized the remodeling? And what would happen to them once the Winter Revels finished?

Chef Perdersen was working away with paper and pencil in his room. The door was open, but I tapped on it anyway, causing him to look up.

"Madame Chalamet! How good to see you again! His Grace isn't with you?" When I said no, his smile grew more sincere. "Not that I would say anything against a friend of yours, madame, but he is not a comfortable man. He asks too many questions and looks at you as if he wants to chop you into tiny bits for a sauté."

I grinned back. "I heartily agree with that assessment. But what I came for today was to talk with your ghostly friend."

He grimaced. "Thankfully, he's been quiet. Let him sleep. He has caused already too much trouble."

"Right now, I need his help to answer some questions about the Lindengaard kitchen. Such as what happened the night you were with Chef Faucher."

"Don't remind me!" he wailed. "My head still hurts from that saucepan."

"Serves you right," said Claude Frossard, who had materialized next to his former lover.

When I joined the Morpheus Society, I learned that many of the beliefs we held about spirits were wrong. Ghosts could materialize during the day, and their forms could appear as solid as a living being. Day ghosts often went unseen by the uninitiated, and spent their time entertaining themselves with minor mischief: moving jewelry, or worse, disappearing your sewing scissors.

I spoke up quickly, as I didn't need the Noise Ghost to cause more mayhem. "Claude, there is something I really need to know about that night. Did anyone, chef or servant, send out a dessert from any of the kitchens?"

Ghosts are horrible about tracking time, but since Claude could link it to the events of Gerhard slinking off to be with his new lover, I felt he could answer pretty accurately. Even so, it took some time for him to search his limited memory before telling me that no one had done so.

"So the king's dessert definitely didn't come from staff?"

"I told His Grace that already," said Gerhard, unwilling to be upstaged by a ghost.

"It's always best to have a double confirmation, and besides, you weren't around. Now, I noticed that when we were served, each chef seemed to use a specific pattern on their plates. Is that intentional?"

Gerhard nodded. "Having a dinner pattern assigned to us has made it easier for the staff to collect the right dishes."

"I'm looking for a specific plate design, and I haven't seen this one so far."

"Describe the design to me, and I will tell you what kitchen it came from."

"It had a pattern of roses around the rim and a bouquet of roses in the middle. Pink and red."

"That isn't one of ours," said Gerhard.

"I know where you can find it," said Claude, rather smugly.

With the information gained from Claude, I searched for Mys Melody Cantrell. That would have been a long quest, except that I located a footman who told me where to find her. The girl was wrestling with a basket filled with laundry. I grabbed a handle to help with her burden.

"Oh no, madame, this is for me to do!"

"I'm bored, Mys Cantrell, so please let me."

Seeing no one else in the hallway who might protest a maid receiving help from a guest, she reluctantly agreed. Besides, I had refused to let go of the basket handle and wrestling it from me would be more unseemly. As we carried it down the hall, she told me, "Everyone downstairs is talking about the coins falling from the air. But I haven't told them the trick, just like you requested."

"I hope there was no trouble for you or the Benard's over it, was there?"

"None! Cynthia's parents loved sticking the coins in the candles in the chandelier above the Marsons' table. And they won't tell either, because they always think the castle servants are snobby, so they love outfoxing them. You see, I'm permanent staff, and the family helps only during special events."

"So they scored a trick over the house staff?" She giggled, nodding. "Now, Mys Cantrell, Chef Perdersen was telling me that there are places in each wing of the house where a servant can make tea or serve up a plate of biscuits. Where is that on this floor?"

"The servant station? We just passed that."

"I didn't see it. Where?"

"His lordship is a clever man, madame. He likes his puzzles." The girl set down the laundry basket and returned down to the end of the corridor. She pushed two fingers into a recess, and the paneling swiveled open like a door to reveal a storage pantry.

I peered into the closet, which was very generous in its size. It held brooms, dustpans, mops, and a serving buffet with a stack of plates and a drawer of silverware. There was a small gas ring where a kettle could be heated.

Searching through the hodge-podge of plates, I discovered one that matched the pattern I sought. "Why are all these plates different?"

"Those are the remains of plates used for the servants, madame. Cast-offs, really, or ones his lordship picked up at auction. He loves a good sale where he can find old books. No one cares if these get broken or lost, so we use them for when guests want something after hours."

She opened some cupboard doors, showing me tins of biscuits, a container for coffee, and others for tea. "After dinner, none of the staff is allowed in the kitchen, so this is how we prepare some refreshment if someone asks without troubling the housekeeper. Terribly put out if she loses her sleep over someone just wanting a little bite, even if they are a lord."

"Who around here would know about these hidden pantries?"

She scrunched her nose, thinking. "The upper house servants like myself. We stock them. Maybe the count's guests? Those that have been here before, I mean."

"I got the impression from Count Westergaard that he didn't have many guests here."

"Oh no, not like the Winter Revels, but back in his mother's time when he was younger, the king's father liked to come here with a few friends. Nowadays it's business folk who deal with wine, or a few friends looking to stay for the winter. It's been a long time since Lindengaard was this busy, madame."

"So these cubbies of goodies were only put back into service recently?"

"Oh yes. I had the devil of a time chasing the spiders out of here."

Something crammed behind the cups caught my eye. I pulled out a long pink ribbon. "Yours?"

"No. I don't know where that came from." Her hand reached

out to take it, but I slipped it into my pocket before she could do so.

"Speaking of guests, did everyone leave for the castle tour?"

"Almost all. The Duchesse de Chambaux is still in her room. Her rheumatism is bothering her something awful. And the Marsons are here. Terribly handsome he is."

Well, I suppose even limp mustaches had their admirers.

"What about Lady Langenberg? Do you know if she is still here?"

"She left with her guardian, Viscount Melgraeve. She's awfully pretty, though he always has a nasty glare on his face. They've visited here many times, because the viscount used to know the count's mother."

"I wanted to retrieve a book I lent her. Where would her room be, exactly?"

Chapter Fifteen

Lady Tulip's room was much nicer than our own, but not as up-to-date as the duke's, which made me guess that Count Westergaard had assigned rooms per our rank. What a fastidious man he was about bloodlines.

Having observed Archambeau's search of Chef Perdersen's quarters, I repeated his method by starting in one corner of the room. I searched the long wall, looking behind paintings and under the chair. When I got to her dresser, I lifted the stack of clothes out, gently picking up the corners and using my hand to feel for any foreign materials hidden between the layers. My fingers ran under and behind the drawers, seeking anything sandwiched there.

I was hoping to find some trace of a letter, note, or a bottle containing poison, but found only the mundane: fine clothes, expensive perfume, silk ribbons, and tortoiseshell hair combs. Unfortunately, neither did I find a diary divulging all a girl's secrets, like how she wanted to murder her godfather for not helping her escape a horrid marriage.

The few books she had brought were social commentaries about the suffering of the lower classes, and her correspondence with charities was about how she could help. All entirely blameless, if rather boring.

Searching the wardrobe, I heard the turn of the handle of her bedroom door. Without thinking, I stepped into the clothespress and pulled the door after me until there was only a thin crack. Once again, I was a peeper.

Seeing who entered, I stepped out of my hiding place

"I've already searched there, Archambeau."

He controlled his start well. "I see our minds go in the same direction."

"You first."

Before answering, he stepped to the door and turned the lock. "When Chef Perdersen inspected the suspicious dessert, he gave me the reasons he and his fellow chefs wouldn't have made it."

"Yes, I know that. Not creative enough."

"Pretty much. Although his exact words were something like he would never serve an uninspiring dish that one could easily buy from any bakery throughout Sarnesse."

"And that led you to a bakery in Vouvant, where Lady Tulip bought such a dessert?"

"She was a patron among several, including you. Matching names to those that were there and those staying at Lindengaard during the Winter Revels makes for a short list of suspects."

"But why focus on Lady Tulip and not her guardian, Viscount Melgraeve?"

"I've already searched his room and found something interesting." From his pocket, he handed me a packet. I read the label out loud: "*Dr. Lilly's patented slimming solution for those who want to encourage health.* A strange coincidence."

"Dr. LaRue told me she tested the Dr. Lilly's compound and found it contained potassium chloride. Another poison that shows a purple flame but gives off no smell. Which one caused the king's distress is unclear."

I nodded in agreement. "She told me the same. We should have

Charlotte test the viscount's sample and compare it to what we found in the king's suite."

"I agree." He returned the packet to his pocket.

"Why would the viscount want to harm King Guénard?"

"He refused to step in and stabilize the market when Melgraeve's shares became worthless. Melgraeve wants the king to wave a magic wand and restore his money. Trust me when I say that if we had such a magic wand, His Majesty's Exchequer would be waving it over the public works department."

"So an excellent motive, along with the means. But how did he gain access? Is that why you are in Lady Tulip's room?"

"She visited the king a few hours before the dessert arrived. They had a very emotional altercation, during which Simon tells me she went to the bathroom to dry her tears. She had access and a reason. Now, why are you here?"

Pulling the pink ribbon from my pocket, I dangled it in front of him.

"This ribbon matches the ones the bakery ties around the cake boxes, and I found it in a pantry closet on this floor, along with a plate matching the one from the king's room. There are no such plates in the chef's kitchens."

I hated to break Lady Tulip's confidence, but an attempt to murder a king was a serious matter and one I could not support with my silence.

"Lady Tulip dropped a similar ribbon in my room when she visited me last, the same night the king was poisoned. She and the viscount probably know about the serving pantries from previous visits. Did you know about them?"

"No. But that isn't a surprise, as I don't wake up in the middle of the night with a yearning for biscuits."

He dropped to his knees and started searching under the mattress. I joined him, examining the pillowcases. "Lord Buckard is trying to force her into marriage," I told him.

"So I heard from His Majesty."

"I was going to ask for your help on the matter."

"Why?"

I tapped the top of his head with the pillow I held. "Because I thought you might have some sympathy for her position."

"Hm. Well, if I was going to have sympathy for every young lady being forced into marriage, I'd die of the vapors. They don't call the match making season the buttons-and-bows auction for nothing, Chalamet."

He stood again and went to the wardrobe.

I threw the pillow down on the bed and stormed over to him, hands on hips. "If you won't help her, I will!"

"By all means," he said calmly.

I stared at his profile while he started going through Lady Tulip's dresses and hat boxes. "How can you be so cold? So cruel?"

"After her marriage, she will take the lover she prefers. That is how those in my class do it." A corner of his mouth smirked. "Did you enjoy overhearing my fight with Valentina?"

Not for the first time today did my face burn to my ears. It was bad enough to have Count Westergaard overhear slurs upon my character, but to know that Archambeau knew that I knew what he'd said was mortifying.

"H-how did you know I was there?" I stuttered.

He gave a chuckle. "Count Westergaard shows that not-so-secret passage to all his new guests. He's very proud of it. And a flash of light behind the peephole told me someone was there."

"But you couldn't know it was me!"

"Your blush confirms my suspicions. See, I am learning how to use your methods to perform interrogations."

We found nothing in the wardrobe, not even my dignity.

Replacing everything, I was about to close the doors again when a key clicked in the bedroom's lock. The handle jiggled, and in the hallway we heard angry voices.

Archambeau's hands around my waist popped me into the closet like a hatbox. Between the wools and velvets, there was little room; I found myself pressed to the duke's chest, his finger on my lips to hush me. I had to restrain myself from biting it.

"Why did you come? I told you I would meet you later. What if my guardian discovers you here?" Through the crack, I saw Lady Tulip enter with Lord Jansen Buckard.

The scoundrel's laugh at Lady Tulip's warning was nasty. "Your guardian could not care less, my little dove. He's already given me permission to do what I will with you. You seem surprised. Do you have any idea how much he owes? How close he is to utter ruin? He needs access to your inheritance as much as I do. With your marriage, he thinks to gain it through me. Won't he be surprised when I don't oblige him?"

My hand automatically went to my pocket, which held my pistol, but Archambeau stopped me from pulling it out. In my ear he said softly, "Wait."

"First, my letters," said Lady Tulip. "You told me you had them? I want all of them. Now."

Letters? What letters? I would have clapped for her defiance, but I was trying to stay hidden in a closet with a man who smelled deliciously of masculine aftershave. The basil and tangerine cologne in my nostrils was making me feel a bit lightheaded.

Something flew by the crack in the wardrobe doors, and a packet of letters landed on the bed. Lady Tulip scrambled after them, putting the four-poster between her and her tormentor. She quickly scanned through them. "I am missing one."

"Yes, you are," Buckard agreed. "The one that is most damning. The one that describes all the secret meetings you attended with those student radicals. How surprised the king would be to discover his little ward rubbing elbows with anarchists."

"I want it now!"

"I'll hand it over when we are married."

"I gave you my word! Please," she begged.

"When you live on the edge, my dear, you learn how little someone's word means." Buckard came across the bed and, grabbing Lady Tulip's arm, brought her down on the bed. He positioned his hand over her throat, holding her still. "Now, a little taste before we seal the bargain with a wedding."

I would have sprung from the cabinet if Archambeau's tight grip on my waist hadn't prevented it. Lady Tulip cried out, "Beast!" before giving him a slap across his face. This didn't seem to dampen his brutishness, for he laid himself on top of her, his hand roaming down her thigh to lift her skirt.

"No," I whispered, closing my eyes tightly.

The duke patted my shoulder, moving me deeper into the confines of the closet. But what I'd mistaken as a comforting hug was instead a chance to pickpocket. He released me and stepping out of the clothespress, raised the man-stopper he stole from me and shot the cur.

The smell of gunpowder burned my nostrils as the shot rang in my ears. Buckard screamed, releasing Lady Tulip, who pulled back to stand quivering against the wall. I leapt out of the closet and grabbing the winter cloak discarded on the bed, draped it around her.

Unfortunately, Lord Buckard wasn't dead. He lay on the bed, gripping his thigh and shooting Archambeau a murderous look. He snarled, "You'll pay for this!"

Archambeau gave him a contemptuous sneer. "Oh, I very much doubt His Majesty will care that I shot the would-be rapist of his goddaughter." To me, he asked, "How is she, Elinor?"

"In shock."

"Can you both make it to your room without being seen?"

"We'll take the servants' stairs. I know where they are."

"If she's returned by now, send Dr. LaRue to me. If not, I'll just let him bleed out. A shame that I missed the femoral artery. Damn, I must be getting rusty."

"If she's not there, I could send the royal physician—"

He cut me off. "He's serves a king, and not a dog."

Chapter Sixteen

My room was vacant of my friend. After settling Lady Tulip on my bed, I wet a face towel using the pitcher at the washstand and gently patted her face, which was warm and now swollen from crying.

"Hush, hush. All will be well. Let Archambeau handle it." My words barely made an impact; still in shock, she continued to weep silently.

The door opened behind me and I heard Charlotte say, "You should have come, Elinor. One snake bite, harmless; two twisted ankles, only one real; and four swoons, one of which resulted in a proposal. And the picnic baskets sent by the count weren't half shabby, either."

"Quick, close the door, Charlotte."

She did so and came over to where Lady Tulip was sitting on the bed. After a quick appraisal of the girl's condition, our mutual gaze exchanged information. She set her bag to the side and clicked open the clasp and soon had Lady Tulip's superficial wounds treated and a healing cream applied. "Get me some water."

With a drink containing a dissolved sleeping powder, Lady Tulip became calmer. I told Charlotte what had happened, and then remembered. "Archambeau wants you to come to Lady Tulip's room because he shot Lord Buckard."

"With any luck, the bullet will be in deep and have to be dug out." Charlotte's eyes gleamed with malicious glee. "Tell me where they are and I'll be off."

After she'd left and with Lady Tulip asleep, I paced the room, wondering what Archambeau was doing and what would happen. Had anyone heard the shot? What would happen to Buckard? Where was Lady Tulip's last letter?

Knowing she was now involved with anarchists and had had access to buying the dessert, her involvement with the king's poisoning looked very black indeed. And she'd probably had access to the Viscount's bathroom to gain Dr. Lilly's patent medicine.

It was about an hour later when Charlotte returned with news. "He's taken the bastard off— back to Alenbonné, where Buckard has lodgings. To collect a letter. He's sent you this note."

Buckard is with me. Keep the lady under watch. I shall return in a day. Be careful, for once in your life.

There was no salutation or signature. I used a candle flame to destroy it. "How did you find Lord Buckard?"

"Alive. But after a long carriage ride in his weakened condition back to the capital, there's always hope for his demise. It really is too bad that His Grace didn't hit the artery. It would make life for everyone so much easier. Especially for any relatives Buckard might have. However, I shall comfort myself, for the bone is badly fractured. If the man lives, he'll probably limp for the rest of his life."

"Well, he can die after we get Lady Tulip's last letter."

"Ah, yes, the letter. I heard them discussing it. Why women write them I do not know. The duke got Buckard to tell him where it was after reminding him of the penalty for a man discovered forcing an unmarried woman."

"Hanging?" I asked. Charlotte made a slashing motion over her groin. "Oh. I see. No, I don't think Buckard would like that."

"Ruin the cut of those tight trousers he likes to wear," Charlotte snorted at her own joke. Removing her coat, she revealed that shirt cuffs stained with blood. She rinsed her hands, using the nail brush to clean under her fingers.

"It makes no sense to me why the marital bed makes forced intimacy acceptable," I said angrily.

"You get no argument from me on that score, Elinor, but the law says otherwise. Men are more concerned with keeping unmarried women pure than keeping married women happy."

"A very good reason not to marry!"

"You won't hear any argument from me there, either. Marriage isn't the proper state for any intelligent woman."

I couldn't agree more, even if a little voice of doubt inside me said that marriage to the right man might be more enjoyable than washing your stockings in the sink on a Sunday evening. A sudden image of domestic tranquility leaped to my mind's eye, only to be spoiled by my fantasy duke saying that after marriage, taking lovers was acceptable.

Charlotte's words shook me out of my thoughts. "While I was working on Buckard, His Grace rounded up a couple of his men to help clear the hall and get him moved."

"Did anyone hear the shot?"

"The duke told a few curious guests in the hall that his pistol had gone off while he was cleaning it."

"Who would believe that?" I said, astonished.

"Would you accuse His Grace of lying? Never mind. You would. But not others." After drying her hands, Charlotte changed into a clean shirt. "He also gave me a packet of Dr. Lilly's patent medicine to test."

"Oh? Good. That would be helpful."

"So, what's the plan for tonight?"

"I think one of us must go down to dinner. Should we toss a royal for head and tails?"

"No one will miss me. My attire makes them question their beliefs too much."

Upset, I demanded, "Has someone been insulting? Who?"

Charlotte laughed. "Don't bother calling them out, Elinor. I've dealt with these narrow-minded fools all my life. They don't prick my pride. I actually enjoy seeing them bluster and stutter, but it would be nice to have a quiet evening reading a book."

I couldn't help but remain troubled by what she did not say. Was she truly unruffled?

"I imagine Lady Tulip will be out for the rest of the evening. Shock tires the body," Charlotte said, looking down at the girl. "You go down and enjoy that six-course dinner. It's what you came here for."

By the time I found my seat at a new table, I regretted that I hadn't been able to convince Charlotte to attend instead, because I found myself at a table with eleven aristos, all determined to talk about subjects I wanted to avoid.

At the end of the table was the Duchesse de Chambaux, with a dress that glittered more than the crystals in the chandeliers above our head, and across from her was Count Christoffer Westergaard, who had given up the idea of a head table in order to join his guests. Viscount Klass Melgraeve was one down and across, and I still found his face and manners boorish. Next to him, sitting directly across from me, was Lady Valentina.

Men might hunt on horses, but ladies shot game while sitting in chairs around the dining table.

"Do tell us all about your recent research, Count. I find it *so* fascinating that all the noble families are linked to royalty." Lady Valentina's smug smile cast in my direction made my heart race.

For the next thirty minutes, I endured a litany of names and excruciatingly detailed explanations of the connections through marriage or progeny of the nobility that sat around the table to the king and each other. My lineage was notably absent.

"Speaking of connections, Count, what do you think of Lady Valdemer taking a lover two ranks below her own? Scandalous. Perhaps you should write her a letter warning her about stooping too low?" Lady Valentina might have been speaking to our host, but her eyes watched mine.

"Perhaps it would be better for her parents to chastise her? It is against custom for a married woman to go down in rank when she chooses her companion." Count Westergaard gave a smirking sideways glance at me as he continued, "Naturally, when a nobly born man looks beneath his class, it can only raise the target of his affections higher."

"Why is that?" asked the youngest woman at the table, a dark brunette who had large, beautiful eyes and an hourglass figure. "It seems most unfair that our own sex cannot bring up our lover in society's ranks if the men can do so."

One man, a sporting type, gave a coarse laugh. "Bloodlines, girl. You do not take a mare and breed her to something inferior. A stallion with the best traits will always improve the get, no matter what he covers."

This crude conversation seemed to amuse the men at the table, but the women sniffed as if smelling something foul. Perhaps this was why when the duchesse finally spoke, her words and tone made the laughter die.

"Men mature slower than ladies. Thus, they have crude impulses, resulting in brief flirtations. It is best to ignore them."

At least the food was good. I made a few ticks on my judging card, and the young man to my right asked what I thought of the first course. Before I could answer, the duke's sister wedged herself into our conversation.

"I wouldn't ask Madame Chalamet. I doubt she can be impartial, since she lives at the Crown Hotel and her favorite chef is in the running for the grand prize."

"You live at a hotel?" asked the gentleman, who had introduced himself earlier to me as Theodoor Visscher.

"Yes, I do. It is very comfortable, and all the décor is up to date, along with en-suite bathrooms that have hot water." Count Westergaard ignored, or didn't hear, my caustic remark.

Thankfully, the second course arrived and talk turned to food. Glasses were re-poured, and Count Westergaard took a moment to do a sales pitch on the vintage from his vineyard. This seemed to go down better than the oration about old family connections.

Further down the table, someone was discussing his experiences at the castle ruins earlier in the day. "It would have been much nicer if the rabble hadn't been pushing and shoving at the top of the wall. At least two ladies twisted their ankles."

"That crumbling wall was about all there was to see," said another.

"You can always tell by a person's manners how well-bred they are," interjected Lady Valentina quickly. "A proper lady knows what to do in all situations. She wouldn't place herself where she wasn't welcome."

I ignored her comment to listen in on a discussion about King Guénard.

"Isn't it just like him to skip out on doing his duties? Although I would have thought eating would be the one thing he would enjoy," said one middle-aged lady with white hair and pale eyes. Her face was blotchy under all the powder and rouge applied to it, making her appear older, which was, I was sure, not her intention.

"Who would have imagined that King Guénard would be too lazy to eat?" said a gentleman with white hair and an enormous nose that was rather red on the end.

A young blond girl said earnestly, "I think you all are being too mean. Migraines are horrible things. If you'd ever had one, you'd know!"

"Indeed, they are," said Count Westergaard, touching the side of his gold-rimmed spectacles. "And I find it disrespectful for us to be speaking so about our monarch. It is a poor jest."

The dark-haired lady pooh-poohed his censure. "We are all

royalists here, Christoffer, but the Winter Revels is his pet project. The least he could do is pretend to show interest, especially since we are allowing these commoners to sit among us."

Another woman, hair so blond as to be almost white, added, "We all have had experiences of the king canceling meetings or declining invitations to our parties. Living far away from the capital, you may not suffer these slights to your dignity here at Lindengaard, but the rest of us are not so lucky. When ruling, he follows his fancies, his whims. King Guénard has the attention span of a butterfly, and his absence tonight proves it."

Leaning over his plate, another man said, "Is it any wonder that there is civil unrest in Alenbonné when the king neglects his duties so? He needs to get a grip on these people before protests turn into riots."

"What do you propose he do about it?" This was from Theodoor Visscher. The man had been almost as silent as I had throughout the meal.

His question sparked a battery of suggestions around the table about what the king should do, some ridiculous and others frightening. It was morbidly fascinating to hear rich people discuss what to do with the rest of us.

"They want lower taxes on exporting goods? I'd raise them higher. Serve them right."

"Naturally, food costs rise in the winter. My workers can't farm when the land is under a foot of snow."

"If he would shut down the printers, it would help. These scurrilous newssheets feed the unrest."

"Expand the House of Commons to match the House of Lords? Ridiculous. King Guénard should stop negotiating with the tradespeople and merchants. What does it mean to have a king if he cannot give orders to these people?"

Count Westergaard tapped his crystal glass with the back of his spoon. "Now, please, let us stop this political talk. I wish to enjoy my dinner, and here comes the last course. Have any of you voted yet?"

Reminded of their duties, everyone pulled out their voting form and started filling it out. Next to me, I heard Visscher mutter under his breath, "Certainly, mysir, let's not discuss the shambles that poses as our government nowadays."

Interestingly enough, Lady Valentina and the Duchess of Chambaux had also been quiet during the political talk. Whether it was through diplomacy or that they held differing opinions, there was no way to tell. Each had an inscrutable face that would do well at the gambling table.

Votes collected, guests were about to rise from the table when Lady Valentina, whose shocked gaze was looking past my shoulder, asked, "Why is there a goat in your dining hall, Count Westergaard?"

Chapter Seventeen

We spun about to see a shaggy, long-haired black goat with curling horns. It must have just come through the door behind it, for it was looking curiously around the room.

Many of the guests rose from their seats; however, one misguided soul shrieked, "Isn't it adorable!" and rushed to embrace her doom. It reared up on its hind legs and charged towards the lady in a manner that I, with no experience of farm animals, would have described as threatening. It head-butted her in the chest and sent her flying over backward.

Proud of vanquishing a lady of gentle birth, the goat strutted about the room, throwing its front legs out stiffly while it prowled the room looking for another victim.

At the count's urging, two of the male servers reluctantly came forward to engage with the creature. However, the goat was more nimble. It feinted, and the men fell forward, as it dashed away with a sideways hop before jumping on a chair and next to a dining table.

"My great-grandmother's crystal!" was Count Westergaard's anguished cry. The count seemed oblivious to the fate of his guests, leaving them to fend for themselves as he directed members of his staff to grab plates and glasses, attempting to save them from the goat's destructive antics.

By this time it was everyone for themselves. The party fractured, and the evening became a pantomime act. The Duchesse de Chambaux and Lady Valentina exited with dignity, even if they were quick-stepping towards the other exit with more speed than usually warranted at evening parties.

My dinner partner, Theodoor Visscher, tried to convince me to leave, but by now I was holding my side from a stitch in my side; laughing so hard it was difficult to breathe. Besides, I didn't want to leave! I wanted to see what would happen.

However, someone with some sense had ousted an intrepid farmhand from his bed if his sagging trousers were any indication. He distracted the horned terror with a couple of carrots. The goat thought for a moment or two, surveyed the room he had destroyed, and hopped down to the floor. Delicately, it reached out with its tiny muzzle and nibbled the green tops of the vegetable.

"Easy now," murmured the farmhand. We held our breath as the man brought out a thin rope from his pocket, bringing it slowly towards the goat's head. The goat drew back its head, just out of reach. The hand stopped. After a pause, once again strong teeth tugged at the greens, trying to dislodge the carrot in the man's hand, but the farmhand had a tight grip. The beast came forward a step to snap the end off, and the hand moved like lightning.

"Gotcha!"

There was a round of applause. But who was it for? For when the little terror left the dining hall, it strutted away with the air of a hero triumphant.

～

With the fun over, I parted from Visscher to seek a servant and arrange for a trundle bed to be delivered to our rooms. Lady Tulip was still asleep when the bed arrived, so I ushered the footmen in with a command to be quiet.

After they left, Charlotte and I were making up the new bed when there was a light tap. Opening the door a crack revealed Mysir Marson; neither he nor his mother had been at the dinner. Stepping outside into the hall, I closed the door behind me.

"My mother begs that you come to her. She's ready to listen."

"Give me a moment."

I went back and explained to Charlotte that I would most likely be gone for a few hours and why. Retrieving my valise, in the hallway I rejoined Mysir Marson, whose face held a conflicted expression as he gazed blankly over my head, deeply distracted.

"Lead on, Mysir Marson," I bade him. As we walked, I asked, "How does the current situation stand?"

He gave a heavy sigh. "She has swung from hysteria to a depressed resignation. She will do what you say, I believe."

Good. My plan was to conduct a séance and bring both parties to the table. Harry clearly wanted to transition and it would be healthier for the widow to let him do so and move on with her life.

At his mother's room in the other wing, he opened the door and ushered me in. "Mother, Madame Chalamet is here now. Let her help."

The widow was sitting in a corner chair, her shoulders slumped, her head bowed. She did not stir at her son's words. Standing behind her was the ghostly form of Harry, the husband and father that only I could see.

Even for a ghost, Harry Marson looked tortured: his body was not whole but tattered as if clawed, and his round face was haggard and his eyes black pits. His was clearly a soul that wanted to transition to the Afterlife; people didn't realize you really could die twice.

"She needs to release me!" the ghost pleaded, his hands imploring.

"Calm yourself. All will be well."

"Thank you, Madame Chalamet," said Mysir Marson, mistaking my comment for one directed at him.

Not bothering to explain, I pulled an embroidered footstool to Madame Marson's side. She still hadn't looked at me, hiding her face behind a tear-drenched handkerchief she was clutching tightly with white knuckles.

"If you wish relief from your husband's ghostly torment, Madame Marson, you must listen to me."

She gave a choking gasp and finally turned her head, showing bloodshot eyes from weeping and skin ravaged by restless nights.

Her voice was hoarse. "The book— and the coins! He's here— I know it! He wins, like he always does. I shall do what you advise, but I do not want my son here. This is a private matter between husband and wife."

Mysir Marson did not want to leave, but after his mother's stubborn assertion that she would do nothing if he was present, he reluctantly agreed.

While they were arguing, I set up what I would need: a small table, two chairs, and a candle between us. From my case, I selected a bottle and a paper packet. The first held a liquid, a custom tincture made from herbs for spiritual protection, that I dabbed on the bottom of my shoes, each palm, my temples, between my eyes, and last, a drop on my tongue.

This would keep me safe from a full-on possession like the one the duke had experienced by the dead student, Bastiaan Hagen. There was a balance between protection and opening the door. So many mediums got this wrong; there was a reason the Morpheus Society put back a portion of our dues for a country madhouse. Mediums who pushed too hard, too quickly, could lose their sanity.

From my bag, I brought out a brass cup and, placing a coal

inside it, lit it. By the time Herkel Marson left, the coal was hot and ready. Opening the paper packet, I sprinkled a spoonful of the herb and resin mixture on the coal. The burning herb let off an earthy, almost bitter smell.

Ghost Talking is a ritual that can only be done with the recently deceased and has nothing to do with direct communication from the dead, but with reanimating the memories of the flesh.

A séance, on the other hand, can be a generic call to any stray ghost to communicate with the medium, or a dedicated summons for a specific spirit residing in the Beyond. Those that have transitioned to the Afterlife we cannot reach; the door to heaven is closed to those of earth.

A medium usually acts as a direct conduit of communication with the dead through a question-and-answer session. The spirit responds with knocks or the flickering of a candle. Another favorite method of mediums is the use of automatic writing. Most likely, Lafayette had used one of these during his initial summoning of Harry Marson.

Tonight's session would be easy, for Harry Marson was standing four feet from me and was eager to communicate.

"Please sit here." I guided Madame Marson back to her seat and took one opposite of her. Reaching out, I invited her to take my hands. With the candle between us, our faces flickered between light and shadow.

She whispered to me, "I'm frightened."

"There is nothing to fear, Christine. I am here as your advocate, but also your protector."

"You don't know—" She stopped herself, her eyes growing panicked.

Because human nature responds to the comfort of talking about the familiar, I asked Madame Marson to tell me about her husband. "Not the things you tell your son, Christine. I am talking about the heart-to-heart confidences you shared as husband and wife."

Even in the dim room with only one candle, I could see a dull blush across her sallow cheek.

"Not the bedroom intimacies, Christine. What was the man like? What was he to you?"

She began hesitantly. "I was barely seventeen when we married. He was a junior in my father's firm, and my father thought well of him and brought Harry home to dinner. I remarked to my family how handsome he was, and since there were no sons to inherit, my parents soon arranged a marriage. We married a month after I turned seventeen."

I breathed in the smoke, feeling lightheaded, my senses expanding, my third eye opening. My quiet listening worked its magic, and she soon grew confiding.

"I was not ready for the reality of married life. My mother told me little other than to submit, and my father cautioned me about guarding myself from becoming a nag. When I turned eighteen, Herkel was born. I almost died on the labor bed. After that, for months, I couldn't look at him. Didn't want Harry around me. He'd touch me and I'd scream."

Her voice still bore the scars of that time. The ghost of her husband tried to put his hand on her shoulder, but though she couldn't see him, she must have felt something, for she shrugged it away. She sighed, shaking her head.

"It was then that I learned to use my womanly arts. The power to control a man with a smile, a frown, or a swoon. If I mentioned feeling sickly, he would shower me with trinkets, new gowns, and once, even commissioned a poem in my name. Whatever I wanted, he gave me. I was young and foolish. It went to my head."

Under the power of the smoke from an herb that removed inhibition, Christine Marson's face glowed, remembering her past victories. However, the wildly flickering candle showed that Harry was not pleased at hearing these truths. Men seldom enjoy learning the secrets we women make for them to appear more than they are.

But soon Madame Marson's smile slumped. "It was just another trap, though. The years passed, and it was too late when I realized I had created a monster! He watched me like a hawk. If I sighed, he'd demand to know what was wrong, how I was feeling. If I didn't want to go to a party because I didn't like the hostess, he would insist I should go to bed early. He treated me as an invalid, even though I had finally recovered from my son's birth. The only time I was free from his eye was when I sent him on errands."

"Like the day he died?"

"Yes."

Admitting it with that one word was like pulling a rotten tooth. Her energy felt immediately healthier once she confessed.

"In a moment, Harry will speak to you through me. Are you ready to hear what he has to say?"

She was clearly frightened, but gave a reluctant nod. "If he will finally leave me alone, I agree, for I only want peace and for him also to be free."

I left open the door and allowed Harry to slip into my body, but the training and my preparation prevented him from seizing full control. Some mediums enjoyed full possessions, but in my estimation, far too many things could go wrong. I did not plan on ending up in a sanatorium.

He opened my mouth and spoke. "Did you never love me, Chrissy?"

Madame Marson cried out. "Oh, Harry, of course I did, but you smothered me!"

"I did it because I loved you. I thought you wanted me to."

"Will you never let me go?"

"I can't leave! You won't let me!"

But even as those words left my mouth, I realized my mistake. Yes, Christine's guilt had formed a Binding, keeping her husband tied to the Earthly plane and unable to pass on to the Afterlife, but she had released that tie with her confession. Harry, though, remained because of his Attachment. His need to look after her had become a responsibility past the grave.

I regained the power of my tongue and told her, "You must convince your husband that you no longer need his help, Christine. He needs to know you can be on your own. He thinks you still need him."

"I don't need him! He can go away!" she said, irritated.

"Understand, madame, for years you did. It is easy to understand why he still believes you still do. Let him know how things have changed."

She grimaced, but eventually complied with my suggestion. "I have a checkbook now, which I balance myself. And I save money. I even paid off the mortgage last month by making double payments these last few years." She said proudly, "I paid off the mortgage last month."

Using my mouth, Harry said, "I don't believe you."

Exasperated, Madame Marson said pertly, "Well, I did! It's through economy. I let the housekeeper go and now I manage the maid and cook."

He asked, dismayed, "You really don't need me?"

"Oh, Harry! I needed you when you were alive. Of course, you were helpful. A bit too helpful. But our time is over. Don't you see?" she pleaded.

POP— Harry's shade was gone. Not just gone, but gone-gone. There was nothing of him in the Beyond. He had moved on to the Afterlife.

I shook myself and, standing up, went to turn up the oil table lamp.

"He's gone?"

"Close your eyes and feel."

She did as I bade and said with wonder, "Yes, there's a difference to the air. To the feeling of it. It's fresher and lighter."

I was glad to give her relief, even if her story was nothing but the details of a wasted life, full of misunderstandings and petty cruelties. Clients weren't always nice young girls in bake shops. They could be selfish old ladies who were hard to love.

I blew out the candle and went to crack open her window. The moon was up, illuminating the vineyards. The air was slightly chilly. I set the brazier on the sill to let the last bit of smoke fly away with the breeze.

To evening's first star, the one that guided the ships on the open ocean, I said, "Godspeed, Harry."

Chapter Eighteen

"Have you forgotten that today is when they post the finalists?" asked Charlotte LaRue.

Returning to our room after the séance, I had found Charlotte already asleep on the trundle, forcing me to take the bed. Now, blinking and rubbing my eyes, I found her standing over me. The doctor wore a comfortable walking outfit of grayish-brown tweed trousers, vest, and coat; it was the color of winter wheat left in the field too long.

"How is she?"

"I'm feeling fine," said Lady Tulip, who was standing at the window, looking out over the vineyard fields. She wore a day dress that covered her from toes to neck, concealing the rough usage of yesterday by Lord Buckard.

Charlotte thumped me on top of my head. "I'm not waiting much longer for you to roll out, Elinor. My stomach is an empty cave and there's a bear inside!"

"I'm getting ready!"

Discarding my covers, I started searching my wardrobe for something to wear. I selected one of my favorite outfits, a deep blue velvet I thought well-suited to my coloring. Charlotte tossed me some rolled-up stockings, which I caught one-handed.

"So, what's the plan for today?" I asked.

"Breakfast," said Charlotte.

Lady Tulip said stiffly, her back to us, "I understand that I'm under some sort of house arrest."

"I'm sorry, but I need to keep you close until the duke returns," I told her apologetically. "But you need not worry about Lord Buckard. The duke took him to Alenbonné."

Her head moved, showing a back-lit profile that concealed her expression. Her voice was remote. "So he lives?"

"The last I saw, he was breathing, but we can always hope that the duke shoots him again," said the doctor cheerfully.

There was a light sigh from the girl at the window. "I do not know if I wish him dead or alive. Once I thought I loved him. Then I hated him. Now I despise him." The back of Lady Tulip's hand swept over her cheek; her fingers shone wet as they dropped to her side. She gave a pitiful wail. "Oh, but how could I have been so blind? So trusting that the outward facade of a man revealed the interior of his heart?"

"How did you meet Lord Buckard?"

"I was doing charity work at the clinic and he bumped into me. Now I wonder if that wasn't deliberate. Making me drop my books? Helping me pick them up? All to make me engage him in conversation, no doubt. What a fool I was."

"You are not at fault for being trusting," I told her, but Lady Tulip ignored me and continued, as if driven to tell us her story.

"Suddenly we started meeting— as if by accident, I thought. Later, by my design. The things I said! But I cannot tell you how loving, respectful, and endearing he was those first few weeks. He gave a sad history of how society had abandoned him, and which prevented him from addressing my guardian directly for my hand."

She swallowed hard. "During our strolls in the park, he convinced me he had the same dedication to helping the lower classes I felt. He told me of secret meetings where others were making change. He escorted me there and soon I fell under their spell. What they said seemed to make perfect sense, until I finally heard them plotting to murder King Guénard. I cut the connection immediately, but it was too late."

"Then Lord Buckard used your letters to blackmail you."

Her pale cheeks gave a sickly blush at my words.

"Do you have that much of a fortune?" said Charlotte, curious.

The sum she named in reply made both of us gape. She waved aside our astonishment, saying, "My fortune has not bought me true love, only pain and sorrow."

"You're not the first woman to be taken in by a cunning bastard," was Charlotte's succinct estimation of the matter. "I see broken hearts with my students every day."

"What's broken can also mend." I gave my friend a warning look. Lady Tulip seemed too fragile this morning for a direct confrontation or a barrage of questions, and besides, I wanted her to naturally confide in us.

Charlotte must have gotten my hint, for she said, "As your doctor, what I prescribe is that we go downstairs, have an excellent breakfast, take a brisk walk through the gardens, and later enjoy a brandy in front of a good fire."

"My guardian would not approve of brandy," said Lady Tulip, finally giving us a watery smile.

"Then we shall be sure to avoid him," said I. "For Lord Westergaard has some mighty fine, well-aged brandy. Or at least that's what I've heard."

∾

Downstairs, we found a posting about who had advanced in the competition. As I had fully expected, Chef Perdersen had made it to the last round. He was one of the final three chefs, including private Chef Beinhouwer from the first round and Chef Cadieux from the third restaurant round. The three would compete in two days, giving them time to design their last menu, train their staff, and order any fresh supplies.

In the garden, strolling side by side, Charlotte outdid herself by providing us entertaining tales about her students. Being Charlotte, though, most of the stories ended with the student being humiliated or expelled from school. Lady Tulip listened politely, but remained sunk in her own thoughts.

We met some of her peers, who asked where she had been the night before. She made polite excuses, and since she did look pale, no one asked further into the matter.

However, it was probably inevitable, I suppose, that we should eventually come face-to-face with the Duchesse de Chambaux and Lady Valentina Fontaine. They greeted Lady Tulip Langenberg warmly and gave me and Dr. LaRue a passing nod. They exchanged pleasantries about the weather, discussed the excitement of the competition (without mentioning the rude appearance of the goat), and wondered if Lady Tulip would be at the final dinner, since they had not seen her last night.

"A maidenly imposition made me miss the dinner, I'm afraid," explained Lady Tulip, causing the duchesse to launch into a list of home remedies for cramps and bleeding that Charlotte reviewed in a more clinical manner.

When we reached a gate that led to the greenhouses, the duchesse and her daughter bade us goodbye, as they had already visited the hothouses and had correspondence to attend to. When they left us, I felt my shoulders ease. The Chambaux family and I would never be friends. If a woman ever contemplated romance with the duke, thinking of the duchesse and Valentina would certainly make her run in the opposite direction.

Before we could enter, I heard someone call my name. This hail was from the young man who had sat next to me last night.

Once he reached us on the path, I introduced Theodoor Visscher to the others.

"Oh, I already know Lady Langenberg." She gave him a nod, accepting the acquaintance. "But may I know who your other companion is?"

I introduced Charlotte with her professional title and where she worked, just in case she started talking about corpses again.

"We were just about to investigate the count's greenhouses," I told him.

"Oh, if you don't mind, let me join you. I have not had the pleasure." He held open the door to the count's greenhouses and, as I passed him by, he said, "I wanted to apologize for my other table guests last night."

"No need."

Charlotte's ears were keen. "Why does he need to apologize for? What did they say?"

"Just typical aristo rudeness to the lower classes, Charlotte." I really did not want to discuss Le beau idéal and their love lives, for it was going to cut close to home for Lady Tulip. To change the subject, I asked Mysir Visscher, "Did anyone discover where the goat came from?"

"A goat!" exclaimed Lady Tulip, finally showing an interest in our conversation.

"The dinner had a surprise guest last night," I told them, filling them in on the appearance of the animal.

"It was eventually discovered that he was from the barnyard, where he was quickly returned," Mysir Visscher told us. "I'm afraid the episode did not amuse Count Westergaard."

"I would think not!" said Lady Tulip. "He is very much a man who stands upon his dignity."

Pompous is what Lady Tulip meant.

"He valiantly rescued his dinnerware," I added, telling them about the mad scramble to remove the table settings before the goat pranced all over them. The mood of our party lightened, and Lady Tulip's manner finally became animated.

With the addition of Visscher to our party, we ended up walking two by two, and naturally the younger members of our party paired with each other. It turned out that Visscher was a naturalist, knowledgeable about plants and their care. He started identifying the specimens, pointing out those of specific horticultural interest. Lady Tulip listened, even asking a question or two.

Behind them, I discussed poisons with Charlotte. One thing about the greenhouse, trees and foliage could hide people wanting a private conversation even when accompanying others.

"While you were dining with a goat last night, I did a few experiments on that packet of Dr. Lilly's the duke gave me. The amount of potassium chloride in it is not high. Relatively harmless. Not the same formula we found in the king's dish."

"You did all that in our bedroom?" I said, astonished.

"I got that servant, Melody Cantrell, the girl from the bakery, to get me things. Stuff from the kitchen and the garden shed. She was very interested and helpful."

"So someone did tamper with the king's bottle?"

"Definitely. I've been thinking about it. I don't think the food had enough arsenic in it to harm him. But potassium chloride could. The standard formula tastes horrible enough as it is, so King Guénard would have ignored the potassium chloride."

"But why taint the dessert?" I asked in a low voice.

Charlotte shrugged. "Perhaps the food was to be blamed when the king grew ill? That fellow Simon begged the duke to let him stay, so I learned a few things. First, everyone knows King Guénard is an outright glutton. Second, the king has his own royal carriage for when he travels by train."

"Is that important?"

"Simon said with all the commotion of arriving that a few pieces of the king's luggage went missing for about ten hours before being found."

I watched as Lady Tulip and Mysir Visscher talked about the hybridization of roses, my mind on more serious matters. "Where could one get potassium chloride, Charlotte?"

"It's used in fertilizer, so I imagine there is some about. Also, any herbalist, chemist, or dispensary could access it, for it's not uncommon. It's not restricted under the Poisoning Act, like arsenic and mercury are."

Our speculative conversation ceased as we exited the greenhouse, for we met Count Westergaard on a tree-lined path that would take us back to the villa.

"Ladies, mysir, I hope you are all enjoying this lovely day."

After sharing compliments on Lindengaard's beauty, Mysir Visscher waxed poetic about the plants he had seen, especially those imported from the tropical climate of Perino. The count preened under the praise.

"My head gardener has done wonders with it after a storm two years ago broke much of the glass. King Guénard sent us several cuttings from his own greenhouses to replace what we lost."

"It's a shame that he hasn't been able to attend the dinners," said Lady Tulip.

"What King Guénard does, or does not do, is of no concern of ours. He is the king," said the count with severity.

Mysir Visscher said, perhaps unwisely, "Perhaps he should look at promoting his pet project, for I saw several carriages piled with luggage leaving this morning. The party for the Winter Revels seems to be shrinking."

The count said stiffly, "The Marson family is returning to Alenbonné, as Madame Marson is feeling fatigued. A few others are disappointed that their chefs have not won and are leaving as poor losers. Not a great loss, I feel."

To soothe his hurt feelings, I said, "I am sure the grand finale dinner will be magnificent for those with the wisdom to remain. Who wouldn't want to stay for the fireworks?"

"Thank you, Madame Chalamet. I agree. Now, I haven't

located the Duke de Archambeau to discuss who will hand out the prizes. Have any of you seen him?"

Feeling Lady Tulip stiffen at the mention of the duke's name, I replied quickly, "He is off on some errand for King Guénard, but I expect him to return from Alenbonné at any time."

Since Lady Tulip dropped her glove at that moment, I was the only one to see the expression on the count's face. The moment passed so quickly that I wondered if I had imagined it, for Westergaard's face had returned to its usual librarian-butler self.

"The king keeps him very busy, I hear. Well, I wish I could walk these gardens all day, but I have other guests to attend to. Ask my man for some of the Perino oranges. He forces them to fruit during winter and they are simply delicious."

Chapter Nineteen

Excusing myself, I left to follow the count. Doing it without being noticed proved easier than I expected, for he barely noticed his surroundings, ignoring several salutations from guests.

When he stopped in the kitchen, I stayed outside the door, hidden by the wall while I waited. "What are you doing?" asked a curious Claude Frossard as he materialized behind me.

"Never you mind."

Count Westergaard didn't stay long before entering the main house, where he started towards the wing which housed the king. I went after him, leaving Claude behind. I deeply regretted not collecting my man-stopper from Archambeau before he left.

On the ground floor, the count went to the end of the hall and opened one of the servant pantries. He closed the door behind him. I took up a post to watch, but when he did not reappear, I decided to investigate. Holding my breath, I pressed the recessed button, but when the secret door opened, I found the space empty!

Rummaging in a drawer, I found a spare candle and matches. With the light, I scanned the closet and found boxes tumbled about. As I stepped over them, my hand fumbled forward and touched the wall. It hinged open and revealed a square space. Inside of it were a series of rungs hammered into the wall. A ladder!

A bit of dirt fell on my face. Looking up, I saw the count's heels a yard or two above me. I hastily blew out the candle, and trusting to touch, put my hands on the ladder and followed him.

There was something eerie about the total silence in the narrow space. Westergaard made no coughs, no muttered imprecations, even when his foot slipped once on a rung and he almost fell. He exhibited nothing of normal frustration, only a preternatural focus on his goal.

I suspected that Count Westergaard had left normal long ago.

He stopped, and I heard him banging on the side wall. It must have been a door or a hatch, for suddenly there was a beam of light above me. He scrambled out; I quickly ascended, hand over hand, foot over foot, to give chase.

Exiting the secret passageway into the royal bedroom, I was just in time to see Count Westergaard knife the sleeping king in the back.

Charging him, I hit his back with the point of my shoulder, bowling him over. As he fell, his knife caught in the thickness of my jacket, making a long rent in the front of it. Quickly, I jabbed him in the eye with my elbow, making him drop it. Westergaard recovered and slapped me hard across the face. I staggered back, reeling. Grabbing his knife off the floor, he dived back into the secret passageway.

Someone picked me up from the floor. It was Archambeau!

"Put some ice on that later, Elinor."

"What?!"

He didn't explain, but let me go chase after Westergaard.

Before following, I checked the bed and found, under the covers, not the king but a mound of blankets which covered sacks of meal. Grain was pouring out of the hole the count had made with his weapon. A trap?

Leaving it, I made for the shaft. My foot found a rung, and I scrambled upward. *Why up?*

I shouted to Archambeau, "Where is King Guénard?"

"Safe!" the duke shouted down to me.

He was gaining ground. In the dim light I saw him attempt to grab the count's ankle, but Westergaard shoved the heel of his shoe into Archambeau's face. The duke had to let go to prevent himself from dropping on top of me.

"Where does this go?" he shouted.

"I would guess the roof!" I called back.

Light came down the shaft as Count Westergaard exited, then Archambeau. When I reached the hole, the duke grabbed my arm and hoisted me out so quickly that I staggered on the terracotta roof tiles, grabbing his tailcoat to steady myself.

Someone hadn't forgotten my man-stopper. It was in the duke's hand as he shouted after Westergaard. "Come down from there!"

Count Westergaard didn't answer. Instead, he scrambled higher, dislodging one or two terracotta tiles. They fell, bouncing against the roof stack and spraying us with broken debris. We both covered our heads, but the sharp end of a chip still scored the duke's cheek.

"Don't trust the roof, Tristan. It's falling apart, like most of the house."

"Stay here."

Of course, I didn't.

Archambeau edged up a valley section of the roof and, by laying flat, pulled himself along with his fingers wedged into the stacked tiles. Using his technique, I followed.

When we reached the peak, we could see Count Westergaard. Now standing where the portico made the front of the house entrance, he was bringing down the king's colors, a flag with the royal coat of arms used to designate when King Guénard was in residence. Once the flag was off the flagpole, the count released it. It flew aloft, carried by the breeze.

"Westergaard!" shouted the duke, but the man paid us no attention, continuing with his task. He pulled something out of a box on the roof and, whipping out the bundle, revealed a flat rectangle of cloth. He ran a new yellow and black pennant up the flagpole.

"What the—?"

"It's his ancestor's banner. The dead ones who should have ruled," I told Archambeau, recognizing the heraldry on the flag from the library display.

"The man must be mad!"

"I fear he is."

"What do you mean?"

"He believes himself to be the rightful king," I explained.

"Is that why he tried to kill King Guénard?"

"Has no one paid attention to his long ramblings about family bloodlines and birthrights? He's a royalist only because he believes the throne is his!"

"That's crazy!"

"As I said."

With his flag flying high, the count was on the move again. Stepping on the ridge of the roof, he started down the line, one foot after the other. He slipped, going down on one knee, his glasses falling off his face to bang down the roof tiles before sliding off the edge.

"This way." Archambeau moved sideways like a crab, his arms above his head, his toes finding invisible crevices. He might be as strong as a sailor climbing a rigging, but my own arms were aching. Still, there was no way back, and no place to rest that didn't risk a fall four stories to the ground.

My foot slipped, and Archambeau grabbed my elbow to prevent a slide that would have ended my adventure. "Steady on,

Elinor. If you wish to run with the hunt, you must complete the course."

The mad count of Lindengaard was far more nimble, or perhaps it was his madness that made him oblivious to the danger. Even with his poor eyesight and thin body, he made it to the other wing. From there, he capered over more tiles, slipping and sliding in a dance like a drunken marionette.

"Where does he intend to go? The game is up," I asked the duke.

"The stables? A horse to flee over the border with? I don't want to shoot him— a fall from here would certainly kill him— but he's giving me little choice."

As Westergaard dropped from view, I shouted at Archambeau, "He's gone down a level, to the breezeway roof that connects the house to the kitchens."

Like careful spiders, we scurried after him as fast as we dared. At the edge, Tristan swung his feet over and lowered himself down, gripping the downspout to steady himself. He reached out his hand to me.

"Be quick, Elinor."

Trusting in providence and the strength of the duke's hand, I went over, eyes closed. Feet hit the tiles, and Tristan's arm steadied me until I gained my balance. Using the strong grapevines climbing up the trellis, we started down.

When Tristan saw I was halfway down and doing well, he told me, "He's raced off to the kitchens! I'm after him!" He jumped down the rest of the way and ran.

It was easy to locate Westergaard from the shouting and screaming. He had gone to ground in the new kitchens, made for the Winter Revels. The kitchen staff stood against the wall, their eyes wide, while Westergaard held a knife to the throat of Gerhard Perdersen.

"The king is dead! I am now your *KING!* Bow to me!" he demanded. "Say it!"

"You are the king," some of them said hesitantly, not understanding what was happening.

"Again! And louder!" Without his glasses to hide behind, you could see the madness in the count's wild, staring eyes.

"You are the king!" A few more had joined in the cheer, while a few were edging towards the back exit.

I had entered from the gardens, right behind Archambeau, who had stopped. He was holding up my gun, trying to line up a shot, but it was a poor thing and not meant for distance.

Archambeau started talking, trying to calm Westergaard down. "Your Majesty, could you please lower the knife? Perdersen can't cook your evening meal if you keep his knife at the man's throat."

"Shut up!" Westergaard told the duke. "You're the usurper's man. Not mine."

"But you killed him," said Archambeau. "Which means I'm now your loyal servant."

I wish he hadn't mentioned killing because someone in the group gave a shriek, and Westergaard's hand jerked, causing the sharp kitchen knife to draw across Gerherd's plump throat, leading a bead of blood.

"Let him go!" screamed Claude Frossard. The Noise Ghost brought a pot crashing down on the back of Count Westergaard's head.

The count slumped unconscious, and the knife dropped from his hand to hit the stone floor, breaking the handle. Free from his hold, Gerhard swam to a nearby kitchen stool, where he collapsed, a hand held to his head. Blood stained the white of his chef's collar.

The duke became busy, marshaling the strongest of the kitchen staff to carry the count off to somewhere he could be contained. Others wept or were talking excitedly about what had just occurred as they exited from the building. Archambeau's commanding voice trailed away down the corridor, and eventually only Gerhard, Claude, and I remained in the kitchen.

Locating a nice bottle of local vintage and two glasses, I filled them and handed one to Gerhard. "Drink up. You deserve it after that nasty shock." He took it with a trembling hand. "Why did he attack you?"

"All I did was tell him to get out of my kitchen! How can they expect me to prepare masterpieces with sightseers in and out of my domain?"

Probably the count had not taken to being told to leave his own property very well. I saluted the Noise Ghost with my glass. "What a hero you are, Claude! Without your quick intervention, who knows what would have happened?"

His face held a mixture of pride and humility; he hovered anxiously behind the barrel form of Gerhard. "How could he attack Chef in his own kitchen? Barbaric!"

"I am finding it hard to grasp what happened," said Gerhard, his hand holding the stem of his glass, trembling slightly. "Why did the count rush in here shouting he was king? Le beau idéal? Who would want to emulate them or their morals?"

It wasn't my place to explain anything. I did not yet know what Archambeau wanted known about this entire incident, so it would be better to hedge.

"It is not your fault and has nothing to do with you or the competition. Once things calm down, I hope to explain things, but for now I'm glad to see you are in one piece. Without Claude, who knows what the outcome would be?"

Gerhard was on his second glass. He gave a burp. "You're right. Without Claude I could be dead! My throat slit from ear to ear! Thank you, Claude. I owe you my life."

"Chef will never forget what you did for him. Will you, Gerhard?"

"Of course not! This horrible day will live in my memory forever. Claude was a lion! A champion! A valiant cavalier." The praise continued, growing more flamboyant in tone with each glass of wine Gerhard consumed.

Over the chef's head, I met the eyes of his ex-lover. "Isn't that what you've truly wanted all along, Claude? Never to be forgotten? To hold a place in Chef's memory that he could never forget, one he could never replace?"

Staring at me, he slowly nodded. If a ghost could have tears in their eyes, he did; he knew this was goodbye for good.

I said kindly, "Lovers are transitory, but not heroes. Their deeds enshrine them and become a legacy that only grows in the retelling. If you stay, you will become like any other, not the hero that Gerhard will remember forever."

Gerhard did not see the last look Claude Frossard gave him as he faded away, transitioning to the Afterlife, but I hoped Claude heard his ex-lover's final declaration.

"Claude always looked after me. He was a pearl, a precious jewel, that I didn't appreciate enough. I will never forget him."

Chapter Twenty

The last dinner, the grand finale, went off without a hitch. I even got to sit with Charlotte, Lady Tulip Langenberg, Lord Theodoor Visscher, and Archambeau.

The duchesse sat at the head table with King Guénard, serving in place of the absent Count Westergaard, who was resting after being sedated in a room with a guard. Thankfully, Lady Valentina was also at another table, far from ours.

"I want to thank my subjects for continuing the Winter Revels in my absence. I may not have been here in person, but I was always by your side in spirit," announced King Guénard. Still pale, he was under strict orders from his physician to sit down as much as he could during the evening and to eat nothing but clear soup. Somehow, I rather doubted that he would follow the advice.

I learned from Archambeau that after the count's dramatics; the king had felt it best to make some sort of appearance to quell rumors.

"Where did you hide him away?" I hissed at the duke. It was the first time I'd had a moment to question him; he had been busy dealing with the fallout of the mad count's rampage.

"I whisked him and his doctor away to a croft on Westergaard's land. They couldn't stay here at Lindengaard. It was far too dangerous."

Pressing my forefinger to my lips, I thought, before saying, "The night of the goat. That's when you did it."

"Yes, a hastily planned misdirection to keep Westergaard busy, so he didn't notice King Guénard being moved out of Lindengaard via carriage."

"Clever. But not as good as my coin shower."

"It was a hasty plan. Can you forgive me for my lack of showmanship?"

"Yes, but next time you should ask for my help. These things need to be conducted with a certain amount of theatrical flair."

"I promise to call upon you the next time I need a distraction."

One nice thing about King Guénard was that he made a brief speech. He kept no one waiting for food was already coming out of the kitchen. The last three chef contestants had risen to the challenge, and the festivities had gone forward despite the antics of Lindengaard's lord.

I waited until our wine and soup had arrived and asked Archambeau in a low voice, "Then you didn't go with Buckard to Alenbonné?"

"No. That blackguard was the least of my worries. His scheme to seize a young woman's fortune wasn't very interesting as a crime."

"So you never thought Lady Tulip guilty?"

I cast my eyes across the table to where she and Visscher had their heads together, discussing reform. The two seemed to have made a connection. While not as handsome as Buckard, his manners were impeccable, and kindness could be a balm to a hurting heart.

"I won't go as far as that. But I reasoned that if Lady Langenberg was guilty, it was because of some manipulation. With Buckard removed, I thought any pressure on her would be gone. Besides, she was under your noticing eye." He paused. "This is the first time I've seen you not pay attention to your food, Chalamet."

I pulled my judging card from under my plate and hastily scored the three soups that were now being taken away to be replaced with the next course of fish. With three chefs, there was a lot of food to digest.

Once the servers retreated from where we sat, the duke continued. "My men took Buckard to Alenbonné under orders that he was to be jailed upon reaching the city. I received a note before this dinner from Inspector Barbier to say that he found her last letter. It's now under lock and key until my return to the city."

"What will you do with it?"

"That's for King Guénard to decide. Lady Langenberg is now his ward, for he has removed her from Viscount Melgraeve's guardianship."

"No wonder the viscount looks miserable. I wonder why the king reconsidered?" I asked.

"Money, Chalamet. Once I explained to him how much she was worth and that he would control it until her marriage, he was more amenable to intervening," said the duke cynically.

Someone across the table asked the duke's opinion on some matter of law. While he answered it, I surveyed the room. Everyone seemed to enjoy themselves, and so far King Guénard had not collapsed, though he seemed to sneak more off his plate than he should have.

When the other dinner companion was satisfied with the duke's explanation, Archambeau returned his attention to me and continued his explanation as if he had not been interrupted. "Everyone knows I am the king's man, and after the failed attempt at assassination, I believed my presence here would prevent another attempt. If the culprit thought me gone, there was a good chance whoever it was would try again."

"But I don't see how you knew it was Count Westergaard."

"I didn't. Unfortunately, there are too many, both high and

low, who would like to see King Guénard dead. Anyone at Lindengaard, including the servants, could have been guilty of it. I could only hope to bait a trap that would entice a rat to creep from his hole."

"Well, I hate to disappoint you, but the count didn't even notice your disappearance! It wasn't until I mentioned you were gone that he hastened to finish his handiwork."

Plates appeared again, interrupting our conversation: roasted duck in cherry sauce; roast beef with mushroom gravy; and a stuffed squab. The portions were small, but it was still a lot of food; I took small bites to savor each taste before scoring my card.

Archambeau was less interested in it. "How did *you* know it was him?"

"I thought him a likely suspect, as Lindengaard was his home, and thus it would be easy for him to arrange things as he wanted. Then, when I told him you were absent, a peculiar expression crossed his face. It is hard to describe, but once you see madness, true insanity, there is no mistaking it. Following him seemed the best thing to do."

"No ghostly insight?"

"Unfortunately not. But why poison the food with arsenic and the Dr. Lilly's with potassium chloride?"

"Ah, so there are things you don't know, Chalamet. Chef Beinhouwer tainted the dessert in an attempt to smear your favorite. He didn't mean to cause any actual harm, just make the king sick to his stomach, so he'd rule against Gerhard."

I clenched the fork and knife in my hand in angry surprise. "What a low thing to do! How did you discover that?"

"I finally tracked down someone who saw Beinhouwer deliver the dessert: a young man exiting another room not his own. When pressed, Beinhouwer confessed to it, though I do not think he had any idea that it would be fatal. He found a canister of the rat killer and sprinkled it on top."

"Despicable," I muttered, stabbing the roast with the tines of my fork. "Why is he being allowed to compete today?"

"Don't worry, he won't win," said Archambeau. "It's best that we carry through as normal for now. Trust me, though, Beinhouwer won't be going back home when this competition ends. A nice cell will cool his hot temper."

"So the count adulterated the Dr. Lilly's compound?"

"It appears so. While we haven't been able to get much sense out of him, it seems he used fertilizer from the estate to taint the bottle. After the count's arrest, a porter came forward and said Westergaard asked him to separate the luggage, allowing him a chance to go through the king's bags and plant the poison."

"But how would an aristo like him know about poison? Did he read a book about it?"

"Apparently, a servant's child last summer accidentally consumed some of the fertilizer. She survived, fortunately. Means, opportunity, and motive."

"What will happen to him now?" I asked.

"I will whisk him away to a place tomorrow, where he shall live under protective custody for the safety of the realm for the rest of his life."

I sighed. "It seems a pity that he can't stay at Lindengaard. It's such a lovely place and is the home to his ancestors. What will happen to it?"

Archambeau gave a slight shrug. "He has no relatives, so it returns to the king. I imagine, eventually, King Guénard will award it to someone." With a mischievous smirk, he added, "Maybe to Dr. LaRue for saving his life."

I smiled. "So there are things you don't know! He's already given Charlotte a stipend for life. That puts her in a quandary; now that she can afford to retire, she admits she enjoys her job at the university too much to let it go, despite having spent the last decade moaning about it."

The Lindengaard staff brought out the last course before the dessert. Savoring a bite of each of the three dishes, I realized it would be impossible to tell which of the three was Chef Gerhard's. My judging would indeed be blind.

Much later, after the dinner, with prizes awarded and when almost all the guests had wandered out to the villa's gardens, Archambeau found me in the count's library.

"Are you hiding in disgrace, since your favorite only took second place?"

"Second place is not shabby at all when you are against such outstanding competition. Remember, he recovered from a threat on his life to win it!" I told him.

I had turned off the gaslights to better enjoy the occasional burst of color illuminating the night sky outside the windows. The planned fireworks were making colorful flowers.

"So, if this is not a diplomatic retreat to hide your disappointment, why are you here? Instead of enjoying the evening outside with your friend?"

Archambeau walked over to where I stood, my hands holding a rather hefty volume filled with color plates of butterflies. The darkness leached our clothes of color, making the planes and angles of our faces gray and black.

"I'm sorting a few things for Count Westergaard. When you told me he had no relatives, I wondered who would think to send his belongings to him. He will need a few comforts where he is going. An asylum isn't a comfortable place."

The duke's eyebrows climbed. "You speak as if you have experience of one?"

"The Society maintains a sanatorium for failed mediums. Those who have lost their minds to the Beyond. I find it a sad place."

He was silent for a moment before replying. "I didn't realize your profession was such a dangerous one."

"When we receive our training, it is required that we all visit the place to see what could happen if we are not careful. It makes for a sobering lesson."

Archambeau picked up a few volumes I had stacked on the corner of the desk and read the titles. "*The Life of the Songbird, Nature's Splendors, The Inner Workings of the Watch*? None of these have anything to do with the count's interest in genealogy."

"Intentionally! He's dwelt too long on those things. For now, his mind needs other food."

"You assume he has some of his mind left?"

"Don't be like that, Your Grace. Where there is life, there is hope."

He cocked his head, looking down at me, his face inscrutable in the half-dark. "I did not realize you had grown so fond of Westergaard."

"I haven't. I actually think he's a bit of a gasbag, with his arrogant assumption that bloodlines make a person better than another. His is a rigid personality, probably incapable of expansion, but I have compassion for even unpleasant people. Their souls are lost twice over. Once because of a lack in themselves, and another because that lack means others find it hard to love them."

He gave me a long stare before passing by me to stand at the window, where he looked up to watch some of the colorful bursts among the stars. He said in a low voice that I had to strain to hear, "A lost soul? No. I cannot give her that."

Was she always on his mind?

Summoning my courage, I said, "I've been wondering why, when we first met, you told me about your wife and how she died. It doesn't seem to be a thing commonly known, even to your closest relatives. Why share that information with me, a stranger?"

His broad shoulders, tailored to perfection in his black tailcoat, lifted and fell. "Unlike Madame Nyght, you showed yourself to be a genuine medium. Once at my home, I imagined you'd hear directly from my dead wife the true ending of her life, whether or not I told you. Sometimes you want to be ahead of the bad news."

I joined him at the window, but instead of looking outside, I turned my back to it so I could watch his face. The cut from the ceiling tile made a short dark line on his chin right next to his older scar.

"If you feared that, why bring me to your house in the first place? It would have been easier to just keep me away."

"I knew from the king that the tiara was missing before unmasking Nyght. When the inspector told me who you were, I thought your knowledge of jewelry would be an asset in resolving the matter. And my hunch proved correct. Anyway, I did not want our relationship started with lies. There are too many lies in the world."

"Don't you mean *your* world?"

He nodded, and a purple burst of light briefly illuminated his face. "You never met my wife, did you? When she was living, I mean?"

"No. Neither living nor dead. However, Jacques did say that her first season was a tremendous success."

He gave a short, brutal laugh. "Every season produces some girl that the men follow with their eyes, and which other poor things want to emulate. They dissect her style, how she handles a fan, her walk, her slippers. The entitled nobility is a small group, well known to each other, desperate for novelty, always seeking someone they can either venerate or destroy. Still, while we thought ourselves wise and experienced, none of us were ready for Minette."

When he stopped speaking, lost in his memories, I prompted, "How so?"

He put an arm over his head and leaned it against the window moulding as if looking for something in the darkness outside.

"She conquered us easily. Even the most jaded ate from her

hand. Perhaps it was her beauty— her shining black hair, the perfection of her skin, the neck of a swan, and the body of a temptress. But that is too easy an excuse. No; while she made experienced men shy with their words, there was still something else. She was a chameleon that changed to suit her audience, providing them with whatever they desired. With her, you felt cleverer, braver, stronger than with anyone else."

"Is that how she made you feel?"

His mouth gave an unpleasant twist, and his harsh tone was all for himself. "Feelings? What do feelings mean in my world? We know only duty and obligation. On the surface, she was an excellent match, a helpmate that I thought would do well with the delicate diplomacy work I do for the king. My mother pushed for the match and reminded me it was past time I started making a family. Thus it was speedily done."

"I am sorry." I laid my hand gently on the arm at his side.

"For what? My stupidity? Gullibility? My arrogance in thinking I actually knew the woman when others did not? Or the self-delusion that I was smart enough to handle her?"

"For your hurt."

He turned to face me. His arm slipped around my waist, bringing us together, chest to chest. A pink illumination in the sky showed me his expression, which was serious, his eyes gleaming wetly. His fingers came up and, feather-light, traced the scar right above my left breast.

"How did you get this?"

His voice was soft, and I leaned toward him. "It was from my father's watch."

"You need to get Dr. LaRue to look at it."

"I will. I promise."

Our mouths came closer, the pull as inevitable as two magnets. The smell of his aftershave; and the rough, masculine touch of his cheek as it came close. The headiness of the moment right before a kiss.

From the door came a bright, girlish voice. "Hello? Is Madame Chalamet in here? My, it's awfully dark in here."

The gas jets were turned up, and his arm fell away. I stood there, dazed by the interruption.

"A servant said I could find Madame Chalamet here," said a tall, gangly girl in her late teens, standing just inside the door. She wore a long coat dusty from traveling, driving gloves, and a sturdy hat. In one hand was a valise, in size and style, a copy of my own.

I cleared my dry throat, now angry. "I am Elinor Chalamet. Who might you be?"

"I'm Twyla Andricksson. Your new apprentice. Sent by Mysir Lafayette, from the Morpheus Society. He said you were overdue for an appointment."

Like the flame of a snuffed candle, gone was the intimate atmosphere. Archambeau gave us both a curt bow, excusing himself. I watched him go, my thoughts going with him.

"I am sure we shall be great friends, for I'm very intuitive and my hunches are never wrong," she informed me. "Your servant at the Crown told me where to find you. She didn't want to, but I insisted. I wasn't going to sit around and wait when we could be working together."

The next day, with the help of Mys Melody Cantrell, we quickly packed to depart. From the Lindengaard maid, I heard that Archambeau had already left with the king's party an hour before.

There would be no chance to meet now. And what of the future? Reluctantly, I thought it was probably for the best that nothing had happened. Dreams did not survive the daylight. I had my life; he had his.

Keeping in mind my promise to him, I asked Charlotte to stay a moment before we followed the trunks downstairs. I unbuttoned the top of my blouse to expose the crescent burn from the watch.

"Would you look at this?"

She examined the area that I indicated, pressing her fingers on my skin. "What do you want me to look at? This mole? It doesn't seem hot. Is it sore?"

I frowned and went over to the mirror. No, the mark was still there, and next to it was a common mole. I pointed again, causing Charlotte to shrug. "Looks fine to me. Typical mole."

Mys Twyla came through our door unannounced. I hastily buttoned up my blouse and shrugged my jacket back up on my shoulders.

The girl said cheerfully, "I didn't unpack last night myself, so I'm ready to go. Are you two ready for the train?"

I had introduced my new apprentice to Charlotte last night, and the doctor, used to irritating students who never stopped asking questions, had taken the girl in stride. As they made their way down the hall, I could hear the two arguing about how long it would take to get back to Alenbonné.

Busy with their chatter, they failed to notice my silence on the ride back to town. Why could Tristan, but not Charlotte, see the mark left by my father's watch when I had dreamed of his death? Why was I saddled with this new apprentice by the Morpheus Society?

And when could I manage a meeting with Tristan again? For despite knowing I should let him go, I knew I wouldn't.

Author Notes

I've always been fascinated by ghosts and have wanted to write a story about them for some time. Pair that with a longstanding love of Sherlock Holmes, that started when I was about nine, and you have the Madame Chalamet series.

My editor, Emma, worked hard by asking all the right questions.

Thank you to the readers who have been so enthusiastic about this series. Your encouragement keeps me going.

BYRD NASH

NOTE: This fantasy world is inspired by 1910 France, but is not a part of it.

For convenience sake, American spellings have been chosen for this fantasy series. For example, instead of grey, gray is used.

For use in this fantasy world, Guardia refers to an individual police officer. Gendarme to the police force, or a group of police officers.

Cast of Characters

- **Elinor Chalamet** (Shall-ah-may)— A Ghost Talker residing in the city of Alenbonné (Alan-bon-ay) in the country of Sarnesse (Sar-nessie).
- **Tristan Fontaine** Duke of Archambeau (Are-shem-bow)— is a member of Alenbonné nobility, **Le beau idéal**. For simplicity, duke is only capitalized when it is used with his title, either Duke de Archambeau or Duke de Chambaux (province title).

Family and Friends:

- **Dr. Charlotte LaRue** (Lah-roo)— Alenbonné coroner and university instructor, and a friend of Elinor's.
- **The Duchesse de Chambaux** (Sham-beau)— Tristan's mother.
- **Lady Valentina Fontaine**— Tristan's sister.

The Crown Hotel:

- **Gerhard Perdersen**— the Crown hotel head chef.
- **Claude Frossard**— Gerhard's former lover, now deceased.
- **Henri Colbert**— the Crown's manager.
- **Pierre**— head waiter in charge of the dining hall at the Crown.
- **Viktor**— the egg supplier to the hotel.

The Winter Revel Chefs:

- **Beinhouwer**— a competing chef (first round and final round). Private service.
- **Chapelle**— a competing chef (first round). Private service.
- **Faucher**— a competing chef (second round). Royal Hotel.
- **Perdersen**— a competing chef (second round). Crown hotel.
- **Cadieux**— (Cad-jou) a competing chef (third and last round). Restaurant.
- **Englehart**— a competing chef (third and last round). Restaurant.

Nobility:

- **King Trygve (Tree-guv) Guénard**— the king and monarch of Sarnesse.
- **Count Christoffer Westergaard**— host of the Winter Revels, held at his manor house, Lindengaard in the village of Vouvant.
- **Lady Tulip Langenberg**— goddaughter of the king and ward of Viscount Klass Melgraeve.
- **Viscount Klass Melgraeve**— The guardian of Lady Tulip.
- **Lord Jansen Buckard**— A member of the nobility.
- **Theodoor Visscher**— a lord who studies botany.

Servants and Helpers:

- **Anne-Marie**— Elinor's servant, a daughter of a sailor.
- **Luca**— the duke's valet.

- **Melody Cantrell**— an upper chambermaid at Lindengaard.

Clients and Ghosts:

- **Claude Frossard**— (deceased) a sou chef at the Crown.
- **Herkel Marson** (a dispensing chemist) and his mother **Madame Christine Marson** and her husband, **Harry** (deceased).
- **Cynthia Benard** and **Melody Cantrell**— two young girls in a Vouvant bake shop. Vernon is Cynthia's (deceased) brother.

Ghost Theory & the Morpheus Society:

- **The Morpheus Society**— an intellectual group of amateurs who study the paranormal using scientific methods.
- **The 3 planes**— Physical where living humans reside; the Beyond, a transitional place where ghosts reside when not in the physical plane; and the Afterlife.
- **Ghost Talking** (not to be confused with a séance)— raises the dead to see their last memories through a ritual used by those trained by the Morpheus Society.
- **Spirit Projection**— this is a moving mind-image (Ghost Talking) that can be created from the recently dead.
- **Noise Ghost**— is a Poltergeist and uses energy from around it to cause trouble.
- **Possession**— an uncommon occurrence and usually short term in duration due to the amount of energy a ghost needs to maintain a connection with a human.

- **Binding**— when a living person holds a soul captive, preventing the dead from transitioning to the Afterlife.
- **Attachment**— when a ghost won't let go of a person or an obsession and exists in the Beyond, refusing to transition to the Afterlife.
- **Death Remembered**— sentimental jewelry for mourning, often holding a photo or lock of hair of the deceased.

Countries:

- **Sarnesse** (Sar-nessie)— a land of rolling hills, with an extensive coastline. Vineyards. Provinces. **King Guénard** (Gie-nar) is the ruler with an elected parliament.
- **Zulskaya** (Zul-sky-a)— the closest neighbor with a large land border. Mountainous.
- **Perino** (Pa-rin-o)— a country of tropical rain forest, separated from Sarnesse by an ocean.

Addresses:

- **Archambeau**— mysir de duke, Mysir de Archambeau (title address) or Mysir de Duke de Chambaux, Mysir de Chambaux (province title). Duke is only capitalized as part of a title. "Mysir de duke" is not an actual title.
- **Madame** (Ma-dahm)— address for any financially independent and professional woman or those who are married. Elinor is 29 and independent, hence the address used for her.
- **Mys** (Miss)— address for financially dependent young ladies, and unmarried débutantes. Typically denotes an immaturity in the title of address, and someone well under the age of 25.

- **Lady**— address denotes a woman of upper class, nobility.
- **Mysir** (my-sur)— address to any man, suitable for all social levels.
- **Lord**— address to any man of clear nobility, or title.

www.ingramcontent.com/pod-product-compliance
Lightning Source LLC
Chambersburg PA
CBHW060949090526
44397CB00061BA/809